Wish for it, Darling

C.K. Franziska

ISBN: 979-8-8840-1880-8

IMPORTANT NOTE

This book ends on a cliffhanger. Please be aware that this genie-reimagining isn't just unicorns and rainbows. While there is spice mixed with humor, the main focus lies on coping with loss through the eyes of a person who has an unhealthy coping mechanism.

Other triggers:

- early parental death

- grief

- forced proximity

- failed engagement

- abandonment issues

- aggressive behavior

- unhealthy coping mechanisms

- manipulation

- explicit sex

GUIDE

Carena Fortunato

CEO of the Indie Inkpot/ Founder of the Word Weaver's Retreat

Evander

Genie/Djinn

Adde

Carena's sister

River

Adde's fiancé/new husband

Atlas

Carena's brother

Olivia

Atlas' wife

Emily

Atlas' daughter

Auton

Carena's father

Chloe

Carena's mother

Leon

Carena's Ex fiancé

Alia

Evander's former lover

Aunt Margaret

A piece of work/ fastest rumor mill in the world

DEDICATION

This is your reminder to tell your significant other you're about to have a new book boyfriend. I hope you are ready to get on your knees and wish for more, Darling.

But first, rub that lamp a little harder for me, will you?

ONE

Frustrated, I slam the vibrator onto the mattress and pull my pants up. I can't do this right now—at least not by myself.

Me: OK, you can come on over.

I hit the send button on my phone.

Who would have thought my time would start ticking the second I turned thirty? And I don't mean death; I'm talking about that inner voice, the longing that tells me to reproduce.

I swore I would never have children, yet it's all I can think of.

Calling my fuck boy over is a horrible idea. Of course, we use protection because I'm not an awful person, and I'm not that desperate—yet. Besides that, I need him for something different, but he doesn't know that yet.

My phone lights up.

Brad: *On my way.*

If I know Brad as well as I think I do, he's already been on his way to my house, circling my neighborhood for a few minutes as he waits for my response.

My phone rings, and I pick it up, not even looking at the caller's name. "You better hurry. I don't know how much longer I can wait for you," I say, my eyes diverting to the lonely, pink-colored vibrator and its accusatory bunny ears pointing at me.

What the hell am I doing? I know exactly that I'll get an orgasm within minutes if I do it myself. So far, I haven't been lucky enough to say the same about a man. Maybe it's because I can't seem to hold on to a relationship longer than a few months since Leon, or perhaps it's because all the men I met believe in the porn they watch and think by just thrusting into a woman, she'll eventually get off on it.

Well, they are wrong.

"Everything is shit," my sister yells through the earpiece, and I jolt up, my mind steering away from my next orgasm.

"What's wrong?" I ask, throwing my blanket over the pink toy to avoid getting distracted.

"You said you ordered red roses. They were supposed to pop in the snow. Guess what I'm looking at? 350 white flowers. White! And to make matters worse, it's not even supposed to snow anymore!" she screams into my ear, and I have to hold my phone away to understand her.

"I ordered red," I reply, rummaging through my brain to recall the phone call with the florist, but my phone keeps buzzing with incoming messages.

My sister huffs. "Can you send me the confirmation so I can show them? Tomorrow is the rehearsal dinner, so I need them first thing in the morning, otherwise, we won't have enough time to set them up."

With a quick motion, I'm on my feet. "About the receipt," I begin, throwing my silken pajamas into the open suitcase beside the door. "It was all verbally. I never had problems with Anita before."

Another message comes in, and the urge to lift my phone away to peek at the sender itches my fingers.

I hear Adde's breath quicken through the phone. She's about to go off. "God damnit. What am I supposed to do now?"

Maybe what you always do. Nothing. Gosh, I wish I had the guts to say that.

"I'll handle it," I answer, looking at the clock on my desk. "But I need to get going," I add, tossing one more pair of fuzzy socks on top of the pajamas. Where I'm going, I'll need them.

"Aren't you supposed to be on your way already?" she asks, her voice laced with an accusatory tone.

After this quickie, that's when I was supposed to leave for the airport, but now I don't have the time anymore.

"I'll handle it," I repeat, zipping the suitcase shut. "You'll have red roses for your big day. Love you. Talk to you later. Bye."

After reciting the last sentences like it's a shopping list, I hang up before my sister can unleash hell on me.

Another wave of messages lights up my phone, and I scroll through them.

Jinelle: What time are you coming back on Sunday?

Cale: Do you want me to book the venue?

Ellie: This manuscript is going to blow your mind. It's going to be a bestseller!

Cale: Never mind. I found your note.

Charlie: The order is coming in on Wednesday. Couldn't get it sooner.

Jinelle: I need your answer as soon as possible.

I close my eyes and take a few deep breaths.

My luck has officially run out.

I had the suspicion yesterday when I received the wrong coffee order, followed by a rejection letter at work, and to top it off, my house key broke, and I had to wait two hours to get in after calling the locksmith. And don't get me started on the chaos at work.

The messed up roses are exactly what I needed to realize that I finally fell out of grace.

Dragging the suitcase down the brand-new staircase, I ignore the loud thuds when it hits one step at a time. My focus falls on my thickest coat in the hallway as my mind replies to every message. They have to wait.

In less than a minute, I have my coat and keys in hand as I

juggle with the doorknob.

"Seriously?" I snarl, rattling it, and eventually, the mechanism releases.

"Carena," Brad says just as I fight with the new key to lock the door to my house that would suit a four-headed family better than a single woman. "Are you going somewhere?"

Slapping my face, I lock it and turn around to face him. "Something came up," I say, shrugging my shoulders. "My sister is getting married, and I ordered the wrong roses. I need to fix it before she orbits the sun."

He looks at me, his handsome face scrunched. Oh, good lord, you rarely find a very attractive man your age who doesn't have any skeletons in his closet. Not that it would bother me, I would cope, but my life is complicated enough to add more loose ends.

"I wanted to ask you if you would like to come with me," I add, plastering the biggest fake smile I can muster.

He cocks his head. "Her wedding? When?"

"Uh…right now. I just have to make a pit stop at my grandma's before we can head out."

He blinks at me like I've just grown a second head. "Today?"

I chuckle. "No, she's getting married in two days."

"But you're saying you want me to go with you *right now?*"

"If you don't mind," I reply, smiling with my teeth.

Our exchange is awkward as hell. I know it's last minute and an unusual request, but come on, be a little more adventurous.

"I'm paying," I add, and I can feel my smile turn into a painful grin.

"You're joking, right?"

"Do I look like I'm joking?"

"Some of us have actual jobs, Carena," he says, shaking his head. "I can't just drop everything and leave. I don't even know where you're going."

Excuse me? I have an actual job. Because of *me*, over a hundred people have *proper* jobs. Being the CEO of the Indie Inkpot, the largest retail bookseller for indie author content, and the founder of the Word Weaver's retreat to bring hundreds of creatives isn't a job or occupation; it's my life.

Brad shakes his head and gives me the same smirk that made me drop my pants for him after our third date. "I didn't mean it like that," he says, reaching for me, but I pull back. "You just caught me off guard."

"So that means you're coming?"

His smirk falters. "Uhm. No. I can't leave."

That's debatable. Since this fling started a few weeks ago, I have gathered little information about Brad. Well, mostly because I was too busy with my legs around his head. Still, I know he does some construction work, which operates mostly on weekdays.

I shrug. "Technically—"

"I can't," he says firmly, cutting me off. "But I hope you have an amazing trip."

Before I can humiliate myself for a third time by trying to convince him to come with me, he turns on his heels and walks back to his beaten-up truck. "Call me when you get back."

The fuck? After he blew me off like that, surely not!

But I guess *never say never*. because when that tiny baby-maker voice returns, I'll need someone to trick my body into believing I'm trying.

"Bye," I reply as I fumble with my keys to unlock my car.

TWO

My grandma's house looks exactly as I remember, with ivy climbing its weathered walls. As I approach the green-colored old house with a charming veranda, my steps echo on the uneven cobblestones. Each stone beneath my feet tells a story of my childhood because, believe it or not, a child's worst enemy is a bumpy pathway. I have too many scars to prove that statement, starting with the deepest one on my kneecap from tripping and falling.

With a jingle of keys hanging from my keychain, I select the right one and unlock the door. The aged lock gives way, and as I push the heavy door open, a rush of air greets me, carrying the unmistakable scent of dust intermingled with my grandmother's lingering perfume. It's a scent that triggers a cascade of memories, transporting me to a time when this house was a haven of warmth and love.

As I step inside, the wooden floor creaks beneath me. The

familiar layout unfolds—the cozy living room where family gatherings took place, the hallway that leads to the kitchen where grandma concocted delicious meals, and the staircase that whispers of ascending footsteps.

The memories flood back as I make my way through the silent house. I can almost hear the laughter, the clinking of utensils, and the rustling of pages from the chair where she used to read.

But today, instead of finding her in the kitchen or on the veranda, my heart breaks again because she isn't here.

I'm the one who discovered her peacefully sleeping in her favorite chair four years ago, an image forever etched in my mind. Back then, I thought she sat down for her usual reading time, which my mother called her *napping hour*. I still can't wrap my head around how she could hold on to a book during her short sleeping sessions.

Pushing aside the emotions that threaten to resurface, I continue my journey through the empty house. The silence is profound, broken only by the sounds of my movements. As I ascend the staircase, I notice the door to the attic is slightly ajar.

That's not how I left it.

One of my siblings must have come here to search for a childhood memory. Since Atlas isn't very sentimental, and Adde's wedding is just around the corner, my money is on my sister. Maybe she was searching for something old she could use for her wedding—my grandma's house is a goldmine for antiques—or perhaps she came here to show her fiancé River where we grew up.

I scan the hallway, my eyes settling on an old wooden ladder tucked away in a corner.

At least that's where I left *that*.

With deliberate movements, I drag the ladder over and pull it apart, its hinges groaning with reluctance as it unfolds before positioning it beneath the door. I gave up looking for the hook to pull the door down years ago, and even though I keep telling myself I would buy a replacement, I still haven't done it.

Mumbling under my breath, I climb the ladder and hook a finger through the cold metal ring to pull on the door. The squeaking hinges send a shiver down my spine as the door groans under the pressure. Pulling it down, I step back onto the ground and push the ladder to the side to unfold the one attached to the door.

"You can do this," I whisper, climbing slowly.

The attic greets me with a dim glow as dust particles suspended in the air dance in the muted sunlight filtering through the small attic window. It's a treasure trove of forgotten items, covered with white sheets that shroud waiting memories of old boxes, faded photographs, and relics of the past.

As I explore the attic's contents, my hands brush against the cool surface of uncovered belongings—a trunk containing vintage dresses, a stack of yellowed letters tied with a ribbon, and a collection of well-read books. Each item holds a story, a fragment of my family's history waiting to be revisited.

But I'm not here for those.

In a corner, I discover an old rocking chair, its once-vibrant upholstery now faded with time. Sitting in it, I allow myself a moment to absorb the atmosphere. The stillness resonates with whispers of my empty heart as if the very air holds echoes of conversations, laughter, and the passage of time I can't get back.

Among the treasures, I see a dusty photo album, its pages fragile with age, and reach for it. Flipping through, I behold images of my grandmother in various stages of life—captured moments frozen in sepia tones. Each photograph pieces her life together.

Still, that's not what I came for.

I need to remember.

I already know those artifacts like the cobblestone beneath my feet outside the house. Nothing has changed since the last time I set foot in it. I'm not here for any old belongings.

I'm here because of my dreams—the vivid ones that make me fly out of bed and question reality.

But deep down, I know I came for nothing. He's not real. I'm aware I made him up.

Yet...

My fingers trace the edges of dusty cardboard boxes, each one a potential portal to my childhood. As I open a particularly weathered box, a rush of nostalgia overwhelms me. Old toys, once cherished companions, lie nestled within the confines of the container. A wave of bittersweet emotion sweeps over me, the echoes of laughter and innocence lingering in the air.

When did I stop playing with them? Can I pinpoint the last time I used the handle to crank my music box or snuggled the brown bear beside it? When did I stop being a child?

My gaze fixates on a golden and green oil lamp among the forgotten treasures. Its presence stirs something deep within me.

There it is.

I remember this lamp from my dreams—vivid and elusive. In those dreams, I'm ten years old again, attempting to clean the lamp to see if I could see my reflection in it, a futile yet compelling endeavor.

I reach for the lamp.

The cool metal feels familiar in my hands as I hold it, memories entwined with the very essence of the object. In my dreams, the lamp holds a mysterious allure, and in the attempt to clean it, something happened that trumped my innocent curiosity.

I groan.

This is stupid. I should be on my way to the airport to sit in the waiting area, slamming down one overpriced drink after another to prepare myself for the family gathering. Not only that, I'm sure I have at least a handful of missed calls and at least twenty unanswered messages waiting for me.

Instead, I decide with a hesitant breath to recreate the ritual from my visions. Slowly, I gently wipe away the layer of dust clinging to the lamp's surface. As the fabric of my shirt moves in circular motions, I can't shake the sense of déjà-vu that envelops me. It's as if I had performed this ritual countless times before, both in the waking world and in the realm of dreams.

Yet, nothing changes with each attempt to bring forth the elusive magic promised by my dreams. The lamp remains ordinary, its surface gleaming but withholding the secrets that my imagination has shown me. A soft, resigned laugh escapes my lips as I realize the absurdity of repeating a childhood dream in the hope of summoning something otherworldly.

I'm insane. I'm fucking nuts!

Placing the lamp back in its spot, I turn around, only to be met with a sight that makes me almost jump out of my skin.

"You could rub it a little gentler next time," the man, who stands right before me, says with a smirk.

I can feel my soul leaving my body as I let out the loudest screeching noise I've ever produced.

What the actual—?

When my reflexes finally kick in, I don't think twice as I send my fist flying straight for his throat. But he grabs my wrist just before I can make contact as if he knew my intentions.

His smile widens as he holds me in place.

The man's golden-brown skin glows in the subdued light, and his dark eyes seem to hold a depth of something I can't pinpoint. His tall frame exudes an aura of mystery, and dark hair frames his face in a way that stresses the intensity of his gaze.

"That's an unusual reaction," he whispers, his smile faltering as his eyes wander over me.

Unusual? What the hell is he talking about? Trespassing and breaking into a house demand retaliation.

"If you don't let go of me, I'll kick your ass," I snarl, looking for any weaknesses. "I have a black belt."

His smile returns. "No, you don't."

How dare he call my bluff?

"Let go of me," I bark, ripping on my arm, but his grip is too firm.

"Promise me you won't try to outsmart me again," he says, squeezing my fist in his large hand, "and I'll let you go."

This is it. I'm going to die here.

Maybe someone will recognize my parked car in the driveway, but it could be days, maybe weeks, because the overgrown bushes shield the house pretty well. How long will it take my family to realize I'm gone? I know they expect me tonight, but I'm probably already six feet under by then.

"I'm Evander," he says, slowly releasing me.

Surprised, I study the man's eyes that hold a familiarity as if I've known him in another lifetime or dreams woven into the fabric of my subconscious.

Yet it's not his appearance that stuns me. Why is he telling me his name? Isn't that unusual for a burglar?

This has to be an illusion, a cruel trick of my mind.

For a moment, I don't speak even though I want to. My mind races, grappling with this surreal encounter. Is he a figment of my imagination or a manifestation of my deepest desires? Is this the sign I've been looking for that I've finally lost my mind?

Breaking the silence, the man speaks in a voice that resonates with a soothing melody. "You seek something, and yet you doubt the possibility of its existence. The lamp, a vessel of dreams, holds more than meets the eye."

My heart pounding, I find myself drawn to his words. As if compelled by an unseen force, I return my attention to the lamp. The man gestures for me to try cleaning it again, a silent encouragement that transcends words.

What am I doing? Why do I feel the need to listen to him?

With uncertainty and determination to stop this madness, I take the lamp in my hands again. This time, as my fingers trace the contours, a subtle warmth emanates from within—the air in the attic shimmers as if touched by an invisible magic. The man observes me with a quiet intensity. And then, as if responding to an age-old incantation, the lamp emits a soft, ethereal glow.

My breath catches in my throat as the boundaries between dreams and reality blur. From the luminous depths of the lamp emerges a subtle bluish-green mist that swirls around him like licking snakes. It feels like a balm for the wounds I carry in the recesses of my soul.

"You're…real," I whisper, pausing my movement. "All this time, you were real."

The man watches me with a knowing smile as my mind rushes through all my memories of him—or rather, his presence.

"How is this possible?" I ask, my mouth dry.

"Which part?"

"You-you are a genie? Am I right?" Saying that word out loud seems wrong because I know better. Mythical creatures are only imaginary tales humans tell each other for entertainment. And don't get me started on genies. They don't exist.

"You already knew that," he says, smirking at me. "But I prefer djinn."

Wide eyed, I shake my head. "I'm sorry. I don't have time for this," I mumble, stepping back. "You can't be here. You need to get out of my head."

What's wrong with me?

Yes, I came here to prove that my luck over the last few years wasn't tied to the lamp I'm holding. I've done a fantastic job concealing the memory of the man talking to me in the attic, calling him an illusion or a childish dream.

But this man, Evander, looks too real to be a deception.

"Just say the words," he replies, his dark eyes lingering on mine.

"What?"

"Set me free. All you need to do is say *the three words* to get rid of me."

Three words? Is he serious?

It takes me too long to realize that he doesn't mean *I love you.* Not that I would say them, but what else is he referring to? *You are free,* or *I free you?* I never noticed how many sentences have three words until my life—sanity—depended on it.

His grin widens. "Say it."

Holding his stare, I immerse in contemplation, my mind swirling with thoughts about genies—excuse me, djinns. As my fingers idly trace patterns on the lamp's surface, I delve into the realm of ancient tales and modern interpretations.

What do I *really* know about them?

Besides the kid's movies, I've watched repeatedly as a child, not much.

They are folklore representing the human yearning for something beyond the tangible. In the recesses of my thoughts, I envision djinns as ethereal beings bound by the confines of lamps or mystical artifacts. Their existence is entwined with magic, granting only three wishes to those fortunate enough to cross their paths.

My musings venture into the dichotomy of djinns. They are caught between the enchantment of their abilities and the limitations of their confinement. I marvel at the idea of beings capable of traversing time and space yet tethered to the vessels that encapsulate their essence. It's a paradox that speaks to the complexities of desire and the intricacies of granting wishes.

As I study him, I consider the moral difficulties often associated with wishes. Djinns become custodians of dreams and arbiters of fate. The consequences of poorly phrased wishes echo in my mind, a cautionary reminder of the delicate balance between desire and consequence.

Three carefully phrased wishes. That's all I have.

But what about their form? He looks too human for something so powerful. And aren't they supposed to be blue?

"Wish for it, Darling, and I'll leave you alone." The grin on his face is so freaking handsome it dismantles every retort I want to give for calling me *Darling*.

Shaking my head to break our stare down, I change my mind. "Don't call me that," I growl, curling my hands into fists.

Three words and all of this will be over. Three words, and I'll hop into my car, mumble to myself on the way to the airport, and spend the next three days explaining to my family why they haven't heard from me in a while and ask why I'm still single.

I've accomplished so much, yet I'm still waiting for my family's approval. It's ridiculous if I think about it, but I can't help myself.

I'm alone—me against the rest of the world.

Unless…

"You grant wishes," I whisper, squeezing my eyes to focus on his face.

He cocks his head. "We already established that."

No. Don't do it, Carena. This is worse than any idea I ever had.

But…I can't show up at the wedding alone. This is my chance to pretend that I'm normal for just a weekend. He's my ticket to show my family that I'm more than just a businesswoman. Plus, if he *is* the man I met years ago right here in my grandma's attic, he's no danger. He could have harmed me back then or all the times I've spent time with her afterward, and he didn't.

"You're bound to me until I release you?"

His wicked smile returns. "More or less."

For crying out loud. He has to stop giving me that grin because my hormones are in overdrive, and I don't have time for games.

I shrug my shoulders to bounce off the hold he has on me. "Then you're coming with me until I figure this out."

"Figure out what?"

"What to do with you," I answer, tugging the lamp under my armpit and out of his reach.

By his facial expression, I can tell that he knows what I'm thinking. Perhaps not that I'm taking him to my sister's wedding, but the part that I know exactly—or rather guess—that I have power over him if I'm in possession of his lamp.

I have three wishes, which will be enough to turn this weekend around. Plus…

"Have you ever done speed dating before?" I ask him, carefully taking a step back.

"I don't think you quite understand who I am."

"I take that as a *no*," I answer, sizing him up. "We have about nine hours to get to know each other before my sister tries to dismantle our spiel. Also, we need to find you something else to wear."

He looks down on himself, and I follow his gaze to the harem pants draping his legs gracefully, a mosaic of rich, earthy colors that shimmer in the morning light. A vibrant green sash cinches his waist, and old arm cuffs encircle his forearms, glinting with an otherworldly brilliance.

I clear my throat when I realize how long my eyes have lingered on his shirtless abs.

His dark hair frames a countenance marked by enigmatic allure—deep, penetrating eyes reflecting the secrets of ages. A short beard adds a touch of wisdom to his visage, and as I lock eyes with him, I feel the weight of untold stories and unspoken wishes hanging in the air.

This should be the part where he asks questions. Instead, he blinks, and the next breath catches in my throat when his attire changes within a heartbeat.

Until a moment ago, I still held on to the tiniest glimmer of hope that I was dreaming.

Shit, I could still be.

I stare at him.

No, I'm not.

"And don't do that again," I croak out, staring at the modern green suit he wears now. "No one can know what you are."

THREE

The walk to my car stretches into infinity. For being a head taller than me, I should be able to hear the wooden planks or the stone path shift under his weight.

I hear nothing.

I'm too terrified to look over my shoulder. What if I imagined it all? Could it be possible that I've been in the attic alone, talking to myself?

Applying more pressure to the lamp wedged between my arm and chest, I fasten my pace. My other hand shakes as I wiggle my keychain out of my coat pocket.

Darn it. I didn't lock the house.

Taking a big breath, I spin on my heels, and a mixture of panic and relief rushes through me when I see the path behind me empty.

It was a dream.

Of course, it was!

Still, my heart is not ready to acknowledge what my brain already knows. I wanted him to be real. Not just today, I've been dreaming of this day since I was ten.

Picking up my composure, piece by piece, on the way back to the veranda, I consider calling Brad one last time to beg him to come with me. I won't survive the weekend alone. Or perhaps I don't have to. Aren't there any other guys I can hit up? Who doesn't want to travel to some cabins in the boonies of Washington State, well, besides Brad?

I let my last hookups run through my mind as I stumble over the path, trying to come up with a potential date…

Nothing. But…

No.

No matter how hard life gets, I'll never call Leon. He's the last person I should be thinking about right now. I shouldn't even have his phone number any longer, yet I do.

Once the door is locked and I'm in the car, I toss the useless lamp into my open purse and stop the key just inches away from the keyhole to look back at my grandma's house.

I thought he was real. In a corner of my brain, I'm trying to decipher if Evander looked anything like the man I saw in the attic as a child. Again, as much as I try to focus on that memory, it's fuzzy and unclear.

"Are we just going to sit here?" a male voice asks from behind me. I hear my neck crack even through the high-pitched scream

I let out as I whip around.

Evander, his brightest smile flashing incredibly white teeth, sits in the back row, buckled up and ready to roll.

"What the fuck is wrong with you?" I yelp, holding my chest to calm my frantic heart. "Why? Why do you keep scaring me like that?"

He raises an eyebrow. "You asked me to go with you."

Sweat forms on my skin as the aftermath of my terror. "I know! How about you don't use your…" I whirl my hands in the air while searching for the correct term.

"Magic?"

Nope, I won't use *that* word.

"Yeah, that," I reply, pressing the key into the starter. "Please try to pretend to be human. Can you do that?"

He leans closer. "Your wish—"

"Please don't say it," I snarl, rolling my eyes.

Am I really this desperate? Taking Evander with me to meet my family is the worst idea in history. Not only will my sister sniff out that something is wrong with our 'relationship', but he's also going to raise suspicion because he's out of this world attractive and doesn't seem to know how to act human.

"Three words," he whispers into my ear, and goosebumps flash over my skin.

I start the car and ignore him.

"I see," he chuckles, tapping his finger against the window.

"So, where are we going?"

"The airport."

He lets out a contemplating grumbling noise, and I bite.

"What is it?"

"I'm trying to remember if I've ever ridden an airplane. I can't say I have."

Oh crap. He is *not* human, which means…

"Do you have an ID or a passport?" What a stupid question. I already know the answer, but it's still worth a shot.

"I'm a djinn, Darling. There's nothing I can't do," he replies as I look through the rearview mirror at him and almost miss the entrance to the highway. With screeching tires, I take a hard left and hear the deserved and furious honk from the driver behind me.

"I know you have limitations," I answer, trying to recall all of them from a movie I know too well. "What are they again? Oh right. You can't kill anyone, you can't meddle with love, and you can't bring anyone back from the dead."

Evander laughs so hard that I can feel it in my bones. "Who told you that?"

As much as I try to suppress the blush rushing into my cheeks, it doesn't work. "It's common knowledge," I whisper, realizing how unprepared I am.

I had years to study genies, but the thought of feeding my childish imagination prevented me from it. All I can now rely on

25

are the few things I picked up randomly.

He chuckles behind me while his finger traces patterns over my headrest. "Don't believe everything you watch on television."

How does he know? I didn't mention how I retained my knowledge.

"So, it's not true?" I ask, blinking a few times.

"I never said it wasn't. You humans are so easily influenced by others."

Anger rushes through me. "What's that supposed to mean?"

He leans forward as far as his seatbelt allows and presses his arms against the front seats. "How much do you know about my kind? Have you met a djinn before?"

The word *you* is loose on my tongue, but I can't say for sure that he was the one I encountered years ago.

"So, there are more of you?" I ask in return to divert his question.

"Oh, Darling—"

I hit the break, and my anger deepens when I see the wave of red taillights before me. "Stop calling me Darling! My name is Carena."

I feel his breath brush against my ear with his following words. "I know you remember me," he whispers, and the familiarity of his voice echoes inside my head.

He used similar words back then, but he said someday we would meet again, and you'll remember me.

"Remember what?" I ask sheepishly, trying to concentrate on the stop-and-go traffic surrounding us.

This can't be happening. If I miss the flight, my sister will flip out and never talk to me again.

He leans back and folds his hands behind his head. "I have all the time in the world," he says, looking out the window. "Sooner or later, you must come to terms with my existence."

That's it.

I whip around to face him. "Why did you stop?"

Slowly, his eyes turn to me. "I thought you don't remember?"

I hit the brakes so hard that I expect his head to hit the seat before him, but he sits there like he's weighing a million pounds.

I bite my inner lip. "I know it was you who made all my wishes come true. But why? And why did you stop now?"

His wicked grin makes my toes curl. "All good things must come to an end."

"That doesn't answer my question. Why did you help me for so long and suddenly stop? Did I do something wrong?"

"How about we reflect on all the wishes I did grant instead of why I halted your recent requests? Don't you remember the shiny unicorn figure you wanted for your eleventh birthday? Or the car to your sweet sixteen? Let's not forget the building you signed for with the brand new sign *Indie Inkpot*."

He said, *halted*. So, he does have more wishes to grant; he just chooses not to.

Yet, something else bothers me more. Everything in life I thought I'd accomplished by myself is a lie. If Evander helped me sign my first lease, what else did he help me with? How many of my accomplishments are actually *mine*?

It doesn't taste very pleasant on my tongue, knowing that since I crossed paths with him for the first time, everything I've achieved is only because of him. I thought I climbed that ladder to become a CEO all by myself, and here he is, Mister *I-grant-all-your-wishes*, smiling into my face.

"Are you alright?" he asks, leaning in closer again.

Am I? I don't know what to feel anymore.

"You're right," I answer, weaving past another car. "Maybe it's time for me to learn from the past and create something independently."

I wish I had said that after we arrived at the airport because right now, I could really use another wish to get through this traffic.

"Then what are you waiting for?"

I glare at him through the mirror again. "Oh, I'm not letting you go just yet. You see, I can't step in front of my family empty-handed. All you need to do is sit through a few hours of the rehearsal dinner, and then I'll free you. Deal?"

"To strike a deal, you must give something in return," he smirks.

Well, shit.

"What do you want?" I'm saying it like I have something to offer, yet I don't. If everything in my life comes from him, how can I repay him?

"I don't know yet," he answers, scratching his beard. "Let's say you owe me a wish in return."

I laugh so hard that I almost snort. "I don't think you understand. Humans can't grant wishes; they're just hot air and dreams that never become a reality."

He clicks his tongue. "Human wishes are so much more interesting than magic. To grant a human wish, you must fulfill a favor and go out of your way. It's more than just a snap of a finger. To grant my wish, the human must do a kind deed for someone else. It's a simple gesture that might not work out, but it's everything for just trying."

I squeeze my eyes together. Did he just say that a simple act of kindness is worth more than magic? It's like a millionaire saying he admires penniless people's money management.

"Yeah, I don't get it," I answer, pressing my lips into a thin line. "But sure, you have one wish."

How freaking calm I am right now is unsettling. I have nothing to lose. All I have to do is try my best to carry through a wish I know I can never fulfill, and in return, I have a date for the rehearsal dinner. This might be the easiest deal I ever struck.

My fingers itch on the steering wheel as my car comes to another halt. I should try it. I should ask him to clear up this traffic jam and be on my way to the airport. But my pride won't let me.

Evander is a wake-up call, and I hear it loud and clearly. Getting used to living without unlimited wishes might sting, but other people do it every day.

If they can, so can I.

FOUR

"You know you would have never made it in time if you hadn't asked me?" Evander asks from the backseat, unbuckling himself.

"Please stop," I command, pulling my suitcase out of the car to drop it onto the concrete.

It was merely a muscle memory when my lips mumbled the wish to end the traffic. I thought nothing of it when I said those words under my breath, and yet, the cars before me picked up speed almost immediately.

"You don't have to be ashamed. I'm happy to help you," Evander replies, picking up my suitcase like it weighs nothing.

That doesn't explain why he didn't grant my other wishes for the last two days. What was different about this one?

"It has wheels," I snarl, pointing at the brand-new pair ready to hit the ground.

He smiles over his shoulder as he walks head-high away from

the car. "I got this."

Oh boy. He might be a djinn, but he has the mindset of showing off his masculinity like a human down to a T.

"You know what I just noticed? It's going to be suspicious if you don't have a bag. Can you…"

Out of thin air, another suitcase appears, dropping onto the one he carries. "Better?"

I exhale deeply while rolling my eyes.

I have eight hours to beat the no-magic rule into his head. "Remember what we said about your *ability*? You need to stop it before someone sees you," I say, looking over the cars to see if his trick went unnoticed.

For now, we're safe.

My gaze wanders back to Evander. Was it really necessary to duplicate my suitcase? Nothing screams more like a desperate attempt to fool everyone than matching clothes and belongings.

"In all my years, I never had someone take me on a trip with them," Evander says, gawking at a family who struggles to stow all their bags back into their car after what seems like a successful trip, according to their sunburns. "I packed lightly," he adds, chuckling as the automatic door slides open.

"I think you're going to regret that soon. You'll need all the clothes you can find where we're going," I answer, already feeling the icy wind of the mountains biting my skin.

"But you said we're going to a wedding."

"A winter wonderland wedding," I clarify without waiting for him to catch up when he comes to a halt.

"That sounds like a horrible event," Evander blares out behind me. "Why would someone do that?"

"I don't know," I mumble, stepping into the terminal. My anxiety eases when I see the board with my plane number. "Let's get you a ticket."

When I approach the ticket counter, sweat forms on my skin. Can djinns lie? What if his magical ID doesn't show up in their system? Or a better question: what if I'm still dreaming?

I clear my throat when it's finally my turn. Pulling out my pre-printed ticket and ID, I approach the smiling lady before me.

"Can you see the man behind me?" I whisper, carefully placing my hands on the counter.

Her eyes turn into slits as she peeks past me. "The gentleman in the suit?"

I follow her gaze, and my eyes land on Evander. "Yes, him."

She slowly nods before her eyes zoom back in on me. She leans in closer. "Ma'am. Are you in trouble? Do I need to call security?"

Looking over my shoulder once more, I check my surroundings for other males wearing suits.

Evander is the only one.

I press my lips together. "I'm sorry. No, I'm fine. You see, I forgot my glasses at home and needed reassurance that I'm not buying a stranger a ticket." I lie with a wide grin on my face before turning to Evander. "Honey? Can you come here?"

"Are you sure you're alright?" the lady asks again before Evander appears beside me. She turns to him. "Sir, may I see your ID or passport?" she asks, grabbing my ticket and ID out of my hand before I can move.

"Certainly," Evander answers, pulling an old wallet out of the inside of his jacket. He produces a real-looking Michigan ID from the inside and hands it over.

The woman's eyebrows knit together as she places our IDs beside each other, her eyes darting from one to the other. "Evander Fortunato?" she looks up from his ID, and I almost choke on my spit.

"Yes?" Evander asks through my coughing fit as I try to regain my bearings and clear my throat.

"Are you freshly married…" she looks down at my ID before continuing, "Carena Fortunato?"

"We are," Evander cuts in, grabbing my hand to curl it around his arm. "I'm so sorry about my wife's strange behavior. We couldn't find her glasses anywhere and didn't want to miss our plane."

The woman raises an eyebrow and studies Evander as if he's her next meal—not in a good way. "May I ask where your ticket is?"

I blew it. We will never get a ticket for him because I was so paranoid about him being real, I already made someone suspicious.

Evander leans over the counter. "I know it's unusual, but my wife insisted on keeping her last name, so I caved. After my name change, we didn't know if my new ID would arrive in time to fly with her."

"Are you aware that you could have used the ID with your maiden name and marriage certificate to purchase a ticket?"

My stomach turns into knots. Now she has us.

"To be honest, I didn't. Since we got married, everything feels like a blur. But thank you so much for pointing it out." He smiles at her. "I would say that I'll remember that detail for the next time around, but I really hope that my first marriage will be my last."

The creases around the woman's brows soften as she begins to smile back at him. "I was worried for a moment that you don't even know this man," she says, looking at me.

"That would be so scary," I fake laugh back, patting Evander's arm.

"Let me see what I can do," she adds, ignoring the discomfort in my smile as she types away.

Ten minutes later, we walk away with a second ticket in hand. My entire shirt clings to my body as we go through security before flopping onto the uncomfortable chairs before our gate.

"Evander *Fortunato*? How did you know my last name?" I ask after the uncomfortable feeling of doing something terribly wrong fades into the background.

He grins at me. "I caught a glimpse of your ID. You blew my original plan to play your brother when you called me *honey*. And by the way, I am as real as you are."

The suffocating feeling surrounding me since I approached the ticket lady—no, since I set foot into my grandma's house—finally subsides with the crushing sense of getting caught. I let go of the thought of trying to understand if he's just an imagination. I've heard about unexplainable events, which must be one of them.

Instead of panicking that something is wrong with me, I should embrace it. For once, I'm not in control of my life, and it feels freeing.

"Can we circle back to the speed dating you were talking about?" Evander asks, ripping me out of my thoughts. "If I'm correct, we only have about seven and a half hours left."

My former self from twenty minutes ago would have freaked out again, but it's useless. In less than eight hours, he will meet my father and my siblings, plus all the other family members I haven't seen in ages.

After responding to all the ignored text messages regarding the Indie Inkpot and pressing Jinelle's incoming calls away, I turn my phone off and scratch my chin. "Where do I begin?"

FIVE

Talking about myself was exhausting, but nothing compared to the turbulent ride that made me feel like this was my last day on earth. The wish to ask for a more joyful experience in that metal can was on the tip of my tongue, yet Evander's knowing grin in my direction made me dig my nails even harder into my arms as I threw every vital detail of my life at him.

"Are you sure you're okay?" Evander asks as I step through the plane's door on wobbly feet. "Let me help you."

"No," I respond, swallowing a burp that could have been more. "I'm fine."

"Just wish for it, Darling, and you'll feel better."

Why is it so hard to accept help? Oh yeah, I already wasted a wish on that stupid traffic jam. What if my wishes are limited now? I can't risk losing them if that's the case.

"I get our rental, and you get our suitcases," I snarl, pressing my purse against my belly.

"These suitcases?" he asks, carrying our twinning bags on his shoulder.

"Oh, my god!" I breathe out, feeling another wave of nausea rumbling through me. "I wish you could just follow simple instructions." When those words leave my lips, I slap my hands on my mouth as if I could shove them back in. "No, I didn't mean that," I plead, looking deep into his eyes. "Please don't—"

"Too late," he replies as the suitcases disappear again. "I guess I'll meet you outside," he adds, strolling past me.

Frantically, I look around to see if the other passengers have seen his magic trick, but everyone is too occupied with themselves to notice.

Relieved, I exhale.

What have I gotten myself into?

As I navigate the bustling lanes of the Seattle airport in the rental Jeep, my eyes dart anxiously over the crowd, scanning the sea of faces for Evander. Anticipation surges through my veins as I round a corner, and there he is—unmistakable amidst the crowd in his green suit, waving with a smile that eases my tension.

Swiftly pulling over to the curb, I pop the trunk of the Jeep. In a seamless choreography, Evander approaches, effortlessly tossing our suitcases into the awaiting trunk. A familiar scent of adventure and reunion fills the air as he climbs into the passenger seat.

It's unsettling how fast I've gotten used to traveling with him. I search for the anxious feeling of interacting with someone I don't know, but after everything I told him on the plane ride, he doesn't feel like a stranger anymore.

I merge into the airport traffic flow, leaving behind the organized chaos of arrivals and departures. The engine's hum and the rhythm of the road synchronize with my excitement as we hit the road.

I'm finally back.

If anyone ever asks me where I want to end up, it's in the woods, far away from civilization and stupidity. The older I get, the more I realize I hate the city. It's loud, gross, and overpopulated.

I wonder what Evander sees when he looks through the window into the world. Does he enjoy the city, or does he prefer silence like I do?

Without shame, I steal glances at him, the green suit a vibrant contrast against the subdued hues of the Jeep's interior.

As we head towards Mt Rainier, the iconic peak looming on the horizon, the cityscape gradually gives way to the open road. A sense of freedom envelopes me, the miles passing beneath the wheels. As we ascend the mountainous terrain, the landscape transforms, offering panoramic views of evergreen forests and snow-capped peaks. The crisp air seeping through the open windows carries the promise of an adventure, a narrative written in every passing tree and rock.

I was once asked why I bought the cabins in the mountains in a state I'd never been to. Back then, I didn't have the correct answer.

Now, I do.

Not a single car has passed us since we entered the winding road on a steep incline. The muted brown tones mixed with the deep green decreased my blood pressure immediately. If it weren't so cold already, I would get out of the car and hike.

This feeling of absolute freedom and calmness is precisely what I'm missing. No phone that continuously rings with orders and deliveries, no junk mail, no hours upon hours sitting in an office for meetings.

"What's holding you back?" Evander asks as I slowly creep around a sharp U-turn.

"What do you mean?"

"I can feel the shift in your demeanor. All the stress of the city is finally falling off your shoulders as if you took a coat off at the base of the mountain."

His words make sense because that's precisely how it felt.

"If you could go anywhere, where would you go?" I ask in return, forgetting for a moment to whom I'm talking to.

Evander presses his head against the window, looking out. "I don't know. It never crossed my mind that I could have a life on my own again."

I almost come to a screeching halt.

What did he say?

"Again?" I blur out, watching him tentatively.

"You think I was born this way?"

"Yeah."

"You're wrong."

"Then please enlighten me," I say, slowly speeding up again.

Evander shakes his head, and a low laugh rumbles through him. "That's a story for another day."

I clench my teeth. "Are you serious?"

"How about an answer for an answer?" he asks, tilting his head. "You go first."

Fine, I can handle that.

"My name is Carena Mia Fortunato, but you already know that by now. I was raised in the house we met by my parents and grandmother and my two younger siblings," I begin, giving him the vaguest information about me.

"I'm Evander."

I stare at him.

He shrugs his shoulders. "That's my name. I wasn't assigned a last name."

"Ok. Since I gave you three facts, I need two more about you."

"After hundreds of years in captivity, I've forgotten how it feels to do everyday human tasks."

"No shit," I reply, recalling the appearance and disappearance of the suitcases as Evander smiles beside me.

"I hate the cold," I add, my eyes glued to the snow-covered peaks in the distance. "But enough about me. You still owe me one more fact."

"I love the smell of vanilla with a touch of lavender," he replies, and I inhale deeply as that scent fills the Jeep as if he had just lit a candle.

Now, that's a random fact I would have never guessed.

Conversation flows effortlessly between us, punctuated by laughter and old memories—well, mostly mine. The Jeep becomes a cocoon, sheltering us from the world outside as we delve into discussions.

I can't recall when our conversation shifted to him asking questions and me answering them.

"You're smooth, you know that?" I ask, estimating that we only have twenty minutes left before the cabins come into view. "I think you now know everything about me. So what about you? Tell me about your past."

Evander shifts in his seat. "It's pretty simple. I wasn't a good human, so I'm being punished for correcting my wrongs until my debt is paid."

The feeling of being safe with a man—djinn—I just met less than twelve hours ago evaporates. We are in the middle of nowhere, without reception for miles.

I clear my throat. "Who did this to you?"

My question should have been: *what did you do?*

"I can't talk about it."

Of course. I would also use that excuse if I were in his shoes. And honestly, it doesn't matter *who* did this to him, because what will I do? Find them and beat Evander's past out of that person?

Gulping my fear down, I twist my head in his direction. "Are you going to hurt me and my family?"

"Oh no, Carena. I'm not a murderer," he laughs, slapping his knee with his hand.

"Then what is bad enough to doom someone to become an eternal servant?"

"I fell in love with the wrong woman," he answers, and my heart stops.

From all the answers I was expecting, this wasn't it, and because I know nothing about love, I keep my mouth shut. There's nothing I can say because I haven't experienced love before.

No, that's not true.

I've experienced the deepest kind of love, and it was soul-crushing enough that I swore never to feel that heartache again.

Still, I wonder what he means. Every day, people fall in love with the wrong person. Maybe because they are already in a relationship, or don't share the same feelings. Neither of those two options is enough to punish someone—unless someone cheated, then I get it.

I confidently navigate the winding roads, each curve a metaphorical turn in the right direction. Occasionally I look over at Evander who gazes out at the landscape, a mix of contemplation and wonder reflects in his eyes.

What did he do?

I want to ask him, but his silence tells me I won't get it, no matter how hard I try to squeeze the truth out of him.

SIX

Reaching a scenic overlook, I park the Jeep, the engine's hum replaced by the hush of nature. I step out onto solid ground, the crunch of gravel beneath my shoes ringing in my ears. The mountain looms above and below, and the cabins stand in a valley surrounded by snow.

I rush back to the Jeep to grab a coat from my suitcase before approaching the overlook's edge. The expanse of nature spreads out before me, a canvas painted with the hues of the setting sun. It's a moment frozen in time, a snapshot of the dream I always had.

Yet this time, a man stands in it, his dark hair tousled by the icy wind.

In the fading daylight, we linger for a moment, embracing the serenity of the mountainous landscape.

"I think it's better if you put a coat on," I say, coming to a halt beside him.

"I don't mind the cold," Evander replies, his eyes roaming over the seven cabins below us. "Are you sure we're in the right place?"

I follow his gaze, and my heart pounds immediately faster when I see the charming wood and stone cabins nestled in a pristine blanket of snow. It's the exact feeling I got when I ventured out here to look at them for the first time. My breath catches as I absorb the winter wonderland, each cabin's memories etched into the wooden walls.

"I rarely come here during snow season," I answer, retreating to the Jeep.

I retake the driver's seat, my fingers gripping the steering wheel. Evander settles beside me, his gaze still fixed on the tableau of cabins below.

Guiding the car down the snowy path, the crunch of tires on fresh snow providing a melodic backdrop, we approach the first cabin—my cabin. A flicker of excitement and nostalgia fills me as I park in front of the welcoming façade. This collection of cabins holds a special place in my heart, often serving as a haven for my Word Weaver's Retreats—a place where creativity flourishes amid the tranquility of nature.

As I step out into the crisp mountain air, my mind dances between the pages of memories and the anticipation of my sister's winter wedding.

Whatever happens this weekend, it won't ruin the image I

have of this place. I've poured my heart and soul into this property to create a spot to wind down and enjoy each other's company while emerging into new worlds through pages.

The cabin's exterior withstands the weight of winter's touch, with icicles hanging like crystalline ornaments and a blanket of snow enveloping the surroundings. Approaching the first cabin, I reach for the door, my anticipation building. Upon entering the cabin, I feel an immediate embrace of warmth, a stark contrast to the chill outside.

However, a warm glow spills onto my face as the door swings open. Surprised, I hesitate for a moment before Evander playfully nudges me forward. With an awkward stumble, I find myself inside, caught off guard by the unexpected scene.

In the cozily lit cabin stands Leon, a mischievous grin spreading across his face. My initial surprise shifts to a blend of confusion and disbelief. The man who had once been a chapter in my life is right before me.

Caught off balance, I stumble, and my face lands pressed against my ex's chest. Awkwardness hangs in the air as I untangle myself from the unexpected encounter. Leon's grin persists with a mix of amusement and a hint of mischief.

"Leon. What are you doing here?" I croak out after I regain my composure.

"It's nice to see you too, Carena," he replies, stepping in my direction. "Your sister told me I would find you in this cabin."

Of course, Adde did.

"This is *my* cabin," I hiss back as my eyes land on the two massive bags in the room's corner that don't belong to me.

"She said it would be better to keep the best man and maid-of-honor in the same building since we will spend most of the weekend together."

Fuck!

My head spins. "You know River?"

"Since Kindergarten," he adds, smiling at me. "I think you even met him once before he started dating your sister."

If I did, I don't recall it. But most of my past is a blur.

Seeing Leon now after all these months is more than upsetting. He was my longest relationship with the most dramatic break-up in history. I thought I would never see him again since our time together was a chapter I closed long ago—at least, it feels like a long time.

But here we are.

My body tenses when two big, warm hands grab my arms from behind. "Are you alright, Darling?"

Oh shit.

How could I forget about Evander?

"Who is that?" Leon asks, his smile dying faster than a mouse in a trap.

"Evander," my djinn says, stepping aside to stretch his hand toward Leon. "Carena's boyfriend. And you are?"

I want to die.

"Your sister didn't mention a boyfriend," Leon replies, shaking his head repeatedly as he studies the man behind me. "She said you would come alone."

Mumbling to myself, I grapple for words—any words. There has to be something I can say to turn this around. But in what direction? Until now, I didn't want Leon back. But here he is, in my cabin. Maybe we can straighten things out.

No. That wouldn't be fair to Evander.

Yet, he shouldn't mind. After all, I dragged him here against his will, if he even has one.

Nope. Can't do it.

Ugh.

Why am I doing this to myself? Just because Leon is here doesn't mean he wants me back.

Or does it?

"She was supposed to come alone," Evander cuts in while my mind goes a million miles per hour, trying to figure out my next step. "That was the plan since I couldn't get out of work, but I guess the stars aligned, and it worked in our favor. Do you need help with those bags?" he adds, pointing at Leon's belongings.

"Stop being an ass," I whisper, bumping into his shoulders as my eyes land on the defined biceps of my ex. Apparently, our break-up didn't hit him that hard because he put his gym hours in by the looks of it.

"No, thanks," he grumbles as he grabs the handles and strolls through the still-open door into the open. The door slams shut behind him without human touch, and my eyes fly to Evander.

"What was that?" I ask, pointing to the door.

"I did you a favor," Evander says with a wide grin on his face. "He's your ex for a reason."

I squint my eyes. "I never said he was my ex."

"You didn't have to. Your face did all of that."

I let out a guttural exhale, and my breath mists the air as I stand in my two-bedroom, one-bath cabin. The crackling sound of a fireplace greets my ears, casting a cozy glow across the living area. Though not large, the main room exudes a comforting atmosphere, with plush furnishings arranged around the hearth. But the second bedroom beckons my curiosity and lets me forget Leon's unexpected visit.

Pushing the door open, I discover the floor-to-ceiling bookshelves lining every inch of the walls, leaving no space for a bed or furniture. The shelves are a mosaic of colors and genres, promising a literary escape that spans the spectrum of imagination. The room seems to breathe stories, the scent of aged paper and ink wafting through the air.

As I trace my fingers along the spines of the books, I marvel at the sheer abundance of tales still waiting to be explored. It's a room where worlds collide, and characters whisper their stories, a sanctuary for solitary retreats into the realms of fiction.

I wish I had thought of bringing a few new books to add to my collection, but today didn't go exactly as planned.

Stepping back into the main room, I catch a glimpse through the cabin's window, revealing a picturesque winter landscape. The hot tub, positioned on a snow-covered deck, emits steam into the frosty air. My eyes light up with anticipation—a relaxing soak in the bubbling warmth awaits me if I survive tonight's meal.

However, familial duties call. Before surrendering to the allure of the hot tub, I need to change my clothes and show my face for a few minutes at the dinner table. It will be fast—in and out within a few minutes.

Without shutting the door, I step into the other room, my chosen resting place that holds a neatly made bed adorned with fluffy blankets and pillows, a haven inviting me to unwind after the long day.

As I enter, I can't resist stealing another glance at the expansive bookshelves before I regain focus and open my suitcase. Evander must have already dropped it off in here. Choosing an ensemble suitable for a family gathering is going to be tough. The mountain air dictates layers, and I embrace the warmth of a cozy sweater and insulated leggings.

As I change, dread of the family reunion bubbles within me.

"Where do I sleep?" Evander asks, and my heart jumps into my throat when I turn toward my reading nook in the corner of my room.

"Shit, Evander! You can't be here!" I scream, covering my already-dressed body beneath my hands.

How long has he been sitting there? How much did he see?

"I didn't force you to undress yourself before me," he replies, his face half-hidden in shadows.

Why didn't I check the room? I guess I'm so used to being alone—in this cabin and back at home—that I forget to keep track of where other individuals are at all times. I didn't check where he went after I ventured into my small library, and I forgot to seek him out before entering this room.

"This room is a no-zone for you, understand?" I say harshly. "This is my room. This is not a one-bed situation. You can have the pullout couch in the living room."

"Ok," he replies, standing up, and my eyes fall on his matching beige fuzzy pullover and slack pants.

I have to give it to him. He has good taste. To pull this fake relationship off, it's going to be perfect because he matches my style—a little too well for my taste.

SEVEN

*E*vander and I trudge toward the most extensive cabin, nestled in the winter's heart landscape. The path beneath our boots, imprinted with fresh marks, whispers of those who have arrived before us, and I'm unhappy to say it looks like a lot of people.

Please, someone, have mercy on me and shoot me now.

When I agreed to come a day early to start the next morning with the wedding preparations, I wasn't told that everyone would be there already.

The setting sun paints the snow-covered world in hues of pink and gold, casting long shadows that stretch toward the cabins surrounding the central one. My breath hangs in the cold air, and with each step, anxiety claws at my chest. Upon reaching the door, I hesitate momentarily, glancing at the man beside me.

The last door I opened had an ugly surprise—no, it was a very good-looking one, but a piece of my past I never wanted to revisit.

"We got this," Evander says, squeezing my shoulder, and with a shared nod, we push the door open, and an explosion of warmth and sound engulfs us.

The rich aroma of home-cooked food wafts through the air with a symphony of laughter and animated conversation. The cabin, the epicenter of my retreats and now for our familial gathering, is alive with the essence of shared joy.

I stand at the threshold, swept away by the vibrant scene within. As I enter, the room comes alive with activity. The glow of string lights adorns the walls, and a large dining table hosts an array of dishes that look pretty inviting. Family and friends mingle, their voices filling the ample space to the rim.

However, as I walk further into the room, a sudden hush ripples through the crowd. Eyes turn toward me, and the lively chatter falls silent. It's as if the very air has paused to acknowledge my presence.

Adde, the radiant, soon-to-be bride, breaks through the stillness. With wide eyes, she rushes forward, her excitement tinged with a hint of curiosity. "Girl! You made it!" she exclaims, enveloping me tightly. But as she pulls back, her gaze shifts to the man who lingers behind.

The air thickens with tension as the Adde eyes Evander. "Who's this?" she asks, her voice laden with a touch of suspicion. "And where's your usual solo entrance? You know, swooping in mysteriously, as always."

I chuckle nervously, feeling the scrutiny of the gathered people intensify. "This," I gesture to Evander, "is someone I'd like you all to meet. Evander. And, well, I thought a bit of company wouldn't hurt this time."

Family members circle us, the atmosphere charged with curiosity. Whispers float through the air like the lightest snowflakes, leaving a palpable tension in their wake. Aware of the scrutiny, Evander offers a friendly smile, but the room remains suspended in a moment of uncertain quiet.

Adde raises an eyebrow, her gaze shifting between Evander and me. "A friend?" she asks, a mischievous glint in her eyes. "You never bring friends. That's new."

"Boyfriend," Evander corrects, holding his hand out to formally greet her.

Attempting to diffuse the tension, I laugh nervously. "Well, it's a special occasion. I thought I'd shake things up a bit."

Adde, ever the spirited one, finally breaks the awkward stare down with a grin. "Alright then, mystery boyfriend, welcome to the chaos of our family. Brace yourself, and let's get you a plate of food before Aunt Margaret interrogates you about your life story."

Laughter erupts again, the room shaking off the temporary stillness, but I know Adde is just the smaller boss we must battle before we get to the last opponent—Aunt Margaret.

As we stand before the buffet-like table, Evander hovers over the delicacies, taking them in individually before he circles back.

"What are you doing?" I whisper, looking over my shoulder to ensure Adde and Aunt Margaret are out of earshot.

"I haven't had actual food in decades," Evander says, slapping a second spoon of mashed potatoes onto his plate as he smiles ear to ear.

After a few seconds, I look at him and realize that my mouth stands wide open. "You don't need to eat?"

"I don't even need water or sunlight, but it's still nice to have them."

I never considered what it must feel like to be *magical*, but watching Evander fill his plate to the rim with food as if he hadn't eaten in forever opens my eyes. He carefully selects from the wide-ranging menu like it's his last meal.

"How long have you—"

I can't finish the sentence because my sister digs her nails into my arm to pull me away. "I just need her for a minute," she says, throwing a big grin in Evander's direction before she drags me with her. "Please tell me he isn't a stranger you picked off the street."

My stomach clenches. If I correct her and say he's a *stranger from grandma's attic*, I don't think it will go well for me.

"I don't think that's any of your business," I answer, pulling my arm back. I'm surprised when my elbow hits a very muscular abdomen.

"We've known each other for quite some time," Evander counters on my behalf, and I'm surprised he's behind me.

The stare my sister gives me is horrifying. Bridezilla is not afraid to use her freshly manicured nails today. "Prove it," she demands, and I swear, if the air was any colder in this room, I could see smoke coming out of her nostrils.

I hold my breath for a moment. "Evander is a…"

Shit. What am I supposed to say? I've given him enough information about myself to survive this weekend, yet I forgot to think about what to say about him. I didn't know she would get upset about me bringing an unannounced plus-one, but I forgot she had been planning her big day since we were kids. Bringing a stranger without an invitation was a stupid idea.

"An attorney," Evander finishes, grinning at me. "I'm sorry for Carena's behavior. I promised her I wouldn't talk about my work while I was here."

Attorney? Is he serious?

Adde tilts her head. "Oh, really? What kind of attorney?"

"I deal with living wills to declare people's wishes."

I have to bite my lip to force my eyes to stay in place and not roll into the back of my head. Well played, Evander, well played.

My sister leans closer and wets her lips as if she can taste his lies. "What else?"

Why is she doing this to me? Is it because she invited Leon in hopes we would get back together? I know it was her doing. Still, it shouldn't concern her who I pick.

"You don't need to do this," I whisper to Evander, shaking my head because I know she's about to strike at him.

"On the contrary, I do," he replies, grabbing my hand after putting his plate on the table beside us. "What else do you want to know?" he asks, returning his attention to my sister.

I'm about to puke because I'm only seconds away from being outed in front of my entire family. I haven't been here for five minutes, and Adde is onto us.

"Let's start with a simple question. What's her favorite color?"

"She would tell you it's beige, but we all know she looks magnificent in maroon."

"Favorite animal?"

"Any cat—big or small. And if you want to know specifically: a Maine Coon."

"Flower?"

"Hollyhock."

"Sports team?"

"None."

"Hobby?"

"You tell me because that's a secret she doesn't even share with me."

My sister inhales.

"I was kidding," Evander adds with a low chuckle. "Did you know she writes stories after sunset in bed when she thinks no one is watching?"

I gasp. How does he know that?

Her eyes dart to me. "Is that true? Are you a writer?"

"Scribbling is a better word for it," I whisper as he squeezes my hand.

Adde builds herself up in front of me. "You, of all people, should know how hard it is to compete in the literature world. At some point, you must accept that those books won't keep you afloat."

What the hell? Is she seriously doing this right now? I haven't even seen my brother or father yet, and she's biting down on me already? I know she's pissed about the flowers and me bringing a plus-one, but that doesn't mean she has to chew my ass up before I even have time to unpack my suitcase.

"You weren't concerned about my career choice when you asked me to pay for half of your wedding," I snap back and cringe when Evander's hand lands on my shoulder.

"I think that's enough for today," he says, gently pulling me away from Adde, who has me in a death stare. "How about we call it an early night?"

An earlier flight back home would be a better idea, but I can't leave. My sister is the biggest pain in my ass, yet she's my only sister. I want to be there during her big day no matter how rough I look after she dismantles me with the ideal life she built

mentally for me.

Plus, this is *my* property!

Two more nights—I can do it.

Tomorrow is the rehearsal dinner, then the wedding with the

after party, and within less than 24 hours after they say I do, I'll

be back on the airplane home.

Evander gently tugs my hand and pulls me into his arms before

he cranes his neck in my sister's direction. "She prefers sunsets

over sunrises because she loves watching the stars. She has a

little dragon tattoo on her ribcage, and she's a fantastic writer,"

he says over the pounding heartbeat in my ears. "I can't wait to

continue our conversation at a later time. It was nice to meet

you."

Without looking at her, I can feel her burning stare on my face.

"Let's go," I whisper, intertwining my fingers with his to pull

him away from Adde before he can say another word.

EIGHT

I thought I'm strong enough, but I can't do it.

"Wait up," Evander says after I rip myself free and storm back to my cabin.

"What was that?" I ask, throwing the plate I'm still holding onto the ground before picking it back up when I remember I'm the one who owns this place. "How do you know so much about me?"

"I'm your djinn, remember?"

"That's not an explanation. How do you know about my stories? And my tattoo?"

I know I shouldn't redirect my anger for my sister's behavior onto Evander, but I haven't told him those things. So how does he know?

I hear his heavy footsteps behind me. "I've been watching you."

I freeze. "That's creepy as shit."

He cocks his head when he comes up beside me. "Not really. It was quite entertaining." His eyes size me up, and my cheeks heat when I realize what he means.

How much has he seen? Maybe he spotted my tattoo while I got dressed in the cabin, but what if he has been watching me without me knowing?

"Eww. So you're a magical pervert?" I snarl, straightening up after picking up the last piece of my now-ruined meal. "Isn't there a rule or something that states whatever you were doing is illegal?"

"Illegal?" He laughs. "Says the woman who used over two thousand wishes in the last twenty years."

I dig my feet into the snow and face him. "You keep track of them?" I hold my finger up. "Wait a second. I thought it was only three."

"That's a misperception. I guess it's wise to put a limitation on your wishes to avoid abuse of our power, but I had too much fun granting yours."

"Why?"

"Why not?"

"Stop answering my questions with questions."

"Then start asking the right ones."

Letting out a guttural sound, I storm the cabin, push the door open, and slam it shut behind me. All of this is too much already, and the actual event, the wedding, hasn't even begun yet.

When I turn around, I cringe when I see Evander standing before me, close to the fireplace. "I'm sorry," he says, taking the plate out of my hand to put it down. "Honestly, I never expected you to come back for me."

I throw my hands in the air. "I didn't even know you were real. For years, I thought I imagined that day in the attic."

"So why did you return if you thought it wasn't?"

"Because I knew that once my luck was running out, it had something to do with that blurry memory in the back of my mind," I answer honestly. "Since I touched that lamp for the first time, whatever I dreamed of became reality. That kept me from returning to find an explanation for my luck. I thought that if I go check it out, I'll disturb what I had going for me."

Evander grins. "Exactly."

"Is that why you stopped? Was it your plan to lure me back?"

"What if I say *yes*?"

I guess he has the right to. I knew I would eventually run out of luck, but I panicked when it finally happened. It's not Evander's responsibility to keep giving and getting nothing in return. He might be a djinn who can do the unthinkable, but he's also a servant against his will.

"I owe you an apology," I say after taking him in. "In the back of my mind, I always knew that our first encounter wasn't a dream, but I thought by ignoring the truth, I could play dumb while abusing your power."

The right corner of his mouth curves into a smile. "You still don't understand. I chose to grant all those wishes because it made me happy. I've kept my eyes on you since you held my lamp for the first time, and I knew I needed to help you."

I swallow hard. "So, what changed?"

"You," he answers, stepping back to give my confusion space.

"Me? That makes little sense."

"It will…soon."

My head spins. Every time I have the feeling I start to understand Evander, he throws me a curveball, and I don't have the energy left to decipher what he means.

"I need a few minutes to myself," I finally say, carefully stepping backward toward my room. "How about we call it a night and start fresh in the morning?"

Evander cocks an eyebrow. "Sure," he says, as my fingers curl around the wooden door to close it.

"If you need anything…" I shake my head. "Never mind, I guess you don't need my help," I press out, shutting the door with a soft click before he can answer.

Leaning against the door, I release a long exhale, a quiet acknowledgment of the mental exhaustion that has settled within me. The muted sounds of Evander walking through the room make my heart ache.

He has done nothing to deserve my anger or resignation, yet I don't know how to say I'm overwhelmed. Perhaps that's the reason I never brought a plus-one with me. Not because I'm unlovable—still, it might play a significant role—but because I'm the person I turn into when I'm around my family.

My eyes sweep across the room, taking in the comforting familiarity of my private sanctuary. Amidst the soft glow of bedside lamps, my gaze lingers on a half-open drawer. Swimsuits peek out from within, a silent invitation that whispers of the outdoor hot tub awaiting me in the snowy embrace of the night.

A spark of realization ignites within me, and a plan forms. Sinking into the plush chair Evander used earlier, I retrieve a book from the nightstand—a companion to accompany my escape into the solitude of the winter night. The cover crinkles softly as I settle into the chair, the pages eagerly waiting for my touch.

Twenty minutes pass as each sentence gently caresses against the canvas of my thoughts. The mental fatigue that has weighed me down dissipates, replaced by the soothing balm of somebody else's words. With a sigh of contentment, I set the book aside, my mind now tuned to the tempting call of warm water.

Quietly, I rise from the chair, my movements deliberate as I tiptoe towards the drawer of swimsuits. My fingers graze the fabric, and anticipation unfurls within me. Silently selecting one, I change into a swimsuit, embracing the notion of an impromptu escapade beneath the night sky.

The bedroom door creaks open when I unlock it, revealing the main room beyond. Evander lies sprawled across a bed adorned with lavish linens that weren't there before. Soft snores punctuate the otherwise hushed room as I stare at him.

I expected to find Evander gone, or at least sleeping in his own 'home', until I realize he can't return to his lamp because it's still inside my purse in my room. It never crossed my mind that djinns also have to rest, but there he is, all six foot three—I'm guessing—upper body undressed and loudly dozing.

Barefoot, I maneuver around his bed, my feet briefly stopping as he shifts before I continue towards the entrance door. The night air is crisp as I step outside onto the snow-covered ground.

Why didn't I bring a towel?

The crunch of snow beneath my feet resonates with the serenity of the wintry night. The cabin's exterior is bathed in the silver glow of moonlight, casting long shadows that dance across the snow.

Arriving at the hot tub, I stare at the protective cover adorned with a dusting of snow as it awaits the touch of my hands. As I lift it away, a gust of steam unfurls into the cold air, creating a transient veil that blurs the distinction between warmth and winter chill.

With deliberate grace, I quietly ease into the water, my bare feet sinking into the bubbling embrace. A delicate shiver travels through my body as the contrast between the crisp air and the heated water envelops me. The night holds a stillness broken only by the gentle murmur of the bubbling water.

Under the canopy of stars, I recline, allowing the warmth to seep into my bones. The cold air kisses my cheeks, and the steam spirals into the night like wisps of ephemeral magic. Once clouded with the day's fatigue, my mind floats in the moment's tranquility. As I immerse myself in the therapeutic waters, the snow around the cabin glistens under the moon's watchful gaze. The world beyond the cabin fades away, leaving only the rhythmic beat of my heart and the soothing whispers of the night.

This is precisely what I needed to regain my strength—a few moments to myself.

I lean back, eyes closed.

That's when I hear the unmistakable sound of approaching footsteps.

NINE

"Mind if I join you?" Leon asks as he steps closer, showing off his trained body in the red trunks he wore on one of our getaways while carrying two towels draped over his arm. A tentative smile plays on his lips as he gestures towards the vacant space in the hot tub. "I saw you sneak out of the cabin and noticed you forgot a towel."

"Don't you have anything better to do?" I reply, huffing in mild exasperation as he approaches even further.

With a resigned nod, I motion for him to step in. Leon lowers himself into the hot water with a subtle splash, trying to find a comfortable distance without encroaching too much on my space. The air is filled with an unspoken tension, and I focus on the steam rising into the crisp night.

After a few awkward and silent moments, he breaks the uneasy stillness. "Look, I know it's been a while, but I've been thinking. I owe you an apology," he says, his gaze fixed on the water.

I sigh, not wanting to dwell on past grievances, especially with my sister's wedding just two days away. "You don't need to apologize. Water under the bridge," I reply, my tone measured.

Leon, however, persists. "No, really. I messed up. I got cold feet, and I shouldn't have handled things the way I did. Breaking off our engagement was a mistake, and I'm sorry for hurting you."

Damn, this hurts.

Memories flood my mind of when I woke up alone in my house with all of his belongings missing and it takes another stab at my heart.

I thought I was over it.

I consider his words for a moment, then nod. "Apology accepted. Let's focus on being civil for the sake of Adde and River."

When I look up, I see the smile on his face that made me fall for him. It's bright and incredibly handsome and stirs something inside me—something I thought I wouldn't feel again.

"Thank you," he whispers as he edges closer, our shoulders almost touching.

The hot tub seems to shrink in size as I try to divert my attention back to the steam rising from the water.

When I woke up this morning, I didn't imagine I would find myself with Leon in a hot tub, surrounded by snow and stars looking down on us. With every inch he moves closer, I can feel his familiarity growing on me.

We all make mistakes, some bigger, some smaller, but what if he really means his apology? What if he came all this way just because he knew I would be here? I mean, he already settled down in my cabin before I even got here.

Just as a semblance of awkward tranquility settles between us, a hairy leg appears out of nowhere in my peripheral vision with a casual confidence that borders on intrusion. Without a word, a man squeezes himself between Leon and me, and I, in fact, know it's a man because his dick is literally on eye level as he steps into the hot tub.

"What the fuck!" I yell, shielding my eyes, but it's too late. The image of an unnaturally beautiful cock burns itself into my memory. "Where are your clothes?"

I hear splashing beside me. "Get your ass out of my face, man," Leon growls, and by the sounds of it, he's already on the opposite side of the hot tub.

Startled, I glance at the newcomer through my fingers, my eyebrows furrowing in mild surprise. Evander, seemingly oblivious to the social dynamics at play, flashes a friendly smile as he settles into the hot tub. Leon shoots him a quizzical look, but Evander remains nonchalant.

Clearing his throat, Evander finally acknowledges Leon. "Oh, hey. Hope I'm not interrupting anything important here," he says with a smirk.

Leon, caught off guard, stammers, "Uh, no. We were just...uh…catching up."

Evander nods, seemingly unperturbed by the subtle tension in the air. Sandwiched between Evander and a corner, I can't help but let out an incredulous chuckle at the situation's absurdity. The hot tub, my escape plan from everything that has happened in the last twelve hours, has transformed into an unintentional battleground of my two unexpected encounters of the day.

"Why are you naked?" Leon asks after a minute, disgust flashing over his face.

"Carena didn't tell me to bring my shorts," he answers, locking eyes with me. "I didn't think it was a big deal because I'm sure we're similarly built."

I choke on my spit.

Is this really happening? Is Evander comparing himself to my human ex-boyfriend? Has he ever seen an average-sized penis before because whatever I was staring at, not even erected, is not comparable to anything I've seen so far?

"Are you okay?" Evander asks, coming even closer, and just the thought of his cock moving closer to me sends a warm feeling through my core.

"I'm fine," I croak out between coughs.

"I'll see you tomorrow, Carena," Leon says, climbing out of the tub while I fight the lump in my throat. Through tears, I watch him march away.

The moment he's out of earshot, I can finally take a breath without having the feeling of suffocating. My eyes form into slits as I take Evander in, who's only inches away from me. "Was that really necessary?"

"Which part?" Evander asks, leaning back to rest his arms on the shell.

"You almost poked my eye out," I snarl, straining my eyes to keep them on his face instead of taking another peek.

"So you liked my entrance?" he teases, and all I want to do is dunk my head into the water and scream.

Why is it so hard to stop thinking about him sitting butt-ass naked beside me? This shouldn't affect me as much as it does.

"I know you did it on purpose," I reply, flashing my teeth at him.

"Can you prove it?"

I bite my lip.

"I can," I muse, watching his eyes land on my lips. "But I have a better idea. I wish," I continue, drawing out every syllable, "that you wear the most ridiculous swimwear known to humankind."

The way his eyes linger on my lips while I form those words is the most intimate feeling without being sexual. It's like his entire being is glued to my words, responding to every letter and every slight shift in my voice.

And as fast as the tension between us started, it disappears. I burst out in laughter as I look past the duck float encircling his chest to the pink mankini now covering his cock.

"Really?" he laughs, and tears stream down my face from laughing too hard when he tries to wiggle his way out of the squeaking float.

"Good luck," I whisper, crawling out of the tub. "And keep the noise down, will you?"

If this costs me a wish, I don't care. It was totally worth it.

I can hear him struggle as I grab the towel Leon left behind for me and run back into my cabin to bring as many doors between Evander, Leon, and me as possible before I do something stupid.

TEN

Sneaking past Evander for a second time won't be an option. I come to that conclusion when I open the door early morning after tossing and turning for hours until I finally fell asleep.

The early morning light filters through the frosted windows of the cabin, casting a soft glow over the room. Tiptoeing across the wooden floor, my steps barely make a sound, and my heart skips a beat when I notice Evander sitting on the plush couch by the fireplace, a steaming mug of tea cradled in his hands. His gaze is fixed intently on the pages of a book, the flickering flames throwing shadows across the familiar words I know all too well. With a sinking feeling, I realize it's one of my books from my personal library—and I mean *personal*.

Heat rises to my cheeks as I silently curse my luck.

"Good morning," Evander greets, his voice breaking the tranquil silence. His eyes lift from the book, meeting mine with a warm smile.

Surprised, I offer a hesitant nod in response. "Good morning," I reply, my voice barely above a whisper.

"This is good," he continues, waving the book in the air.

I can feel sweat forming on my skin.

"From all the books you could have picked from, you chose that one?" I ask, freezing mid-motion.

His smile widens. "I was intrigued since it's the only book in your collection that doesn't have an author."

Yes, because *I am* the freaking author—I guess *wannabe author* is a better term.

As I march in his direction to rip my book out of his hands, a sudden knock on the cabin door shatters the moment. With a furrowed brow, I turn towards the entrance, my heart pounding in my chest. Evander remains seated, his gaze fixed on me with a quiet intensity.

The door swings open with a creak, revealing a figure silhouetted against the morning light. The air whooshes out of my lungs as my father steps into the cabin, his presence a bittersweet reminder of the past. It has been over a year since I have last seen him, and the ache of longing and loss wells up within me.

"Dad," I whisper, my voice tinged with emotion as I rush forward to embrace him. His arms envelop me in a warm hug, the familiar scent of his cologne washing over me like a comforting blanket. Tears threaten to spill from my eyes as I bury my face in his shoulder, the weight of my grief pressing heavily upon my heart.

"You look just like your mother," Auton murmurs, his voice thick with emotion. The words hang in the air like a poignant echo of the past, stirring memories of a time I don't want to travel back to. My heart clenches at the mention of my deceased mother, the pain of her absence a constant ache in my soul.

As we pull apart, my father's gaze fills with concern as he takes in my sad face. "How have you been, my rosebud?" he asks.

I force a smile, pushing aside my grief for the moment. "I've been...managing," I reply, my voice wavering slightly.

Auton's expression softens with empathy as he tries to brush a stray tear from my cheek. "You don't have to be strong all the time, rosebud," he says gently. "Sometimes, it's okay to let yourself feel the pain."

Nodding, I take a deep breath, the weight of my heavy heart easing slightly under my father's comforting presence. I shouldn't feel like this, not after almost twenty years have passed since my mother didn't wake up after going to sleep that night.

"I'm so glad you're here," Auton continues, looking past me. I can see the exact moment his eyes land on Evander because they double in size as he takes him in. "Adde told me you brought a special someone with you." His surprise tone in the last words hurts more than it should.

"Dad, that's Evander. Evander, that's my father, Auton," I cut in quickly as Evander puts the book down, stands up, and walks in our direction, his hand stretched towards my father.

"Pleasure to meet you," he says, shaking my father's hand. "I've heard so much about you."

"I wish I could say the same," Auton replies, staring at me before his gaze turns back to Evander. "I also heard about my daughter's interrogation. She's been on edge the last couple of weeks, and since Carena kept you such a well-hidden secret, she was unprepared."

"You mean rude?" I snarl, rolling my eyes.

"Unprepared," my father repeats, letting go of Evander's hand.

It doesn't surprise me that my father defends my sister. After all, she can't do anything wrong and always gets her way. I used to wonder if his expectation of the eldest child would be the same if one of my younger siblings were born first, or if it's just my personality he thinks can handle more than the other two.

But who am I to judge? I used the powers of a djinn for two-thirds of my life without even knowing it.

Auton clears his throat. "I just wanted to stop by real quick since I missed you last night."

"We were just getting ready to head your way," I lie as I shove the guilty feeling of forgetting my father down. It's not like I didn't want to see him, but the memories of supporting him through his grieving process while I bottled up my own emotions have taken its toll on me.

"I mean, if you guys are ready, we can grab a bite to eat and tackle the setup for the wedding. The sooner we finish, the more time we have to rest."

Rest.

That's a word I try to avoid at all costs. I can't rest. If I do, my past catches up to me. Well, part of it is currently grinning at my father like a dog waiting for a bone—Evander.

"Let's go," Evander says, clapping his hands together. "I can't wait to get this party started."

That makes only one of us.

A flurry of activity greets us as we approach the large cabin where the wedding preparations are in full swing. Family members bustle about, their voices mingling with the rustle of decorations and the occasional burst of laughter. The air is thick with anticipation, the promise of a fairytale winter wedding hanging like a delicate veil over the scene.

"So you *do* have a soft side," Evander whispers into my ear. "I knew it."

"You're slowly becoming my least favorite person," I growl back through smiling teeth in case someone watches us.

Taking in the chaos before me, I know exactly why my father

came looking for me. Sure, he wanted to see me, but he also knows I can't stand clutter. My minimalistic living style is very sterile compared to my sister's tendency to hoard mismatched decor, sentimental pieces that have no connection to our family or anything she has experienced in life, and the feeling of filling her house with random shit.

Does it make her happy? Maybe. But it drives me insane.

With my father by my side and Evander offering a supportive smile, I dive into the midst of the preparations, ready to lend a helping hand wherever needed.

I navigate through the bustling crowd; my keen eyes quickly assess the situation. Some family members and friends are busy arranging the white flowers my sister didn't want, others are hanging twinkling lights, and still more are setting up tables and chairs for the reception. It's a symphony of organized chaos, each person playing their part in bringing the vision of the winter wedding to life.

With a sense of purpose, I set to work organizing different groups of people, delegating tasks, and ensuring everything runs smoothly. With Evander at my side, we work tirelessly, our efforts fueled by the thought of earning ourselves a breakfast, since Adde closed the kitchen until everything is set.

Together, we transform the cabin into a wonderland indoors and outdoors. String lights twinkle like stars overhead while swathes of tulle and satin drape elegantly from the rafters. Tables are adorned with glittering centerpieces, and delicate snowflakes hang from every available surface.

As the morning wears on, Adde finally emerges from the chaos and approaches me, a furrow of concern marring her brow. "We still have the problem with the flowers," she says. "The florist insisted on delivering the white roses instead of red, and they're not what I told you to order."

A knot forms in my stomach when I realize I still haven't called Anita, the florist. It was on my agenda when I left my house, but everything changed when that damn door didn't want to shut.

"Don't worry," I reassure her, a determined glint in my eye. "I'll take care of it."

Stepping outside into the crisp winter air, I pull out my phone and dial Anita's number. With a calm but firm tone, I explain the situation and request that the flowers be changed from white roses to red for tomorrow's wedding. After a few minutes of negotiation, I hang up the phone.

"What's wrong?" Evander asks as he closes the door behind him.

Watching him tentatively, I rub my lips over each other before answering. "How does this wish-thing work?" I prob as I stuff my phone back into my pocket.

"Is that your way of asking me how many wishes you have left?"

Ugh. I should have expected a counter-question.

"I messed up the flower order," I say, deciding that beating around the bush won't work out.

"So…you want me—"

"No. I mean, yes." I exhale. "Seriously? I don't know. I just called the florist, and she said there's no way she can gather the amount I need. Now, I don't know what to do."

I understand my sister is flustered about the color, but at least she has roses. Who cares what color they are?

"Wish for it, Darling," Evander says, and the hair on my neck prickles at his words.

Why is it so hard to say those words? They used to be second nature to me, but since I stumbled upon Evander, wishing has gotten a different meaning.

"I can't," I reply, recalling how fast my words turned into reality last night. My wish barely left my lips before it materialized around his chest, and…no, I don't want to think about the mankini and what it was covering up, nor the consequences of that wish. Do I owe him a second wish?

Evander takes me in. "Consider it done."

I throw my hands in the air. "But I didn't tell you what flowers Adde wants."

"Red roses. Very unoriginal, in my opinion, but I'm not the bride."

I can't agree more with him, but that's not what I'm hung up on. First, how does he know? And second… "Is there something I can give you in return?"

If I'm known for something besides being alone and organized, it's that I hate being in debt.

"How about another wish?"

My eyes wander over the mountains. Another wish. It doesn't seem fair as payment since there's nothing I can give him he can't get himself. But this is my sister's wedding. I can't let her down.

"Deal," I answer, looking straight into his eyes as I contemplate if I owe him now two or three wishes.

Returning to the bustling cabin, I find Adde waiting anxiously. "It's all taken care of," I say and relief washes over my sister's face. "Red roses will be delivered first thing tomorrow morning. But in return, I finally need something to eat."

"You're the one who messed the order up."

I roll my eyes. "That doesn't mean you have the right to let me starve."

Plus, this is still my cabin, and I can use the kitchen whenever I please. I wish I had the guts to say that aloud, but I won't survive another misstep with her.

ELEVEN

As the sun sets on the horizon, painting the landscape in a warm, golden glow, I stand back and survey the room before me. The cabin has transformed into a fairytale winter wonderland, every detail meticulously planned and executed with care. As the final touches are put in place and the last guests arrive for the rehearsal dinner, I know my mother would have loved tomorrow—a celebration of love, family, and the beauty of winter, her favorite season.

It's hard to decipher if my sister picked snow as the theme for her wedding because she enjoys it too or if her subconscious picked it to have the feeling our mother is with us.

Perhaps I'm the only one remembering that detail about her since I was ten when the ambulance arrived that morning. I'll never forget my sister's face. Her six-year-old brain wasn't ready to understand what was going on. She reveled in the attention of the first responders and then in the attention our family got until the funeral.

"I think you need a break," Leon says, bumping my shoulder with his. "Let's get some fresh air."

I shouldn't accept his offer since most people in this room know about our short-lived engagement. Additionally, Evander is technically my boyfriend in my family's eyes.

But this room is shrinking with each moment I stare at the decorations.

"Ok," I mumble, my eyes searching for Evander, and a smile rushes over my face when I see him entertaining Aunt Margaret. Maybe I should be worried since she's a bloodhound for drama and secrets, but Evander was good enough to get my sister off my back, and since then, she hasn't returned with more questions about our relationship.

"Five cents for your thoughts," Leon says as we step outside.

That sentence furls around me like a favorite smell. Throughout our relationship, he used it daily, and if he actually paid out, I would be rich.

"It's nothing," I whisper, wrapping my arms around my waist to keep myself warm.

Leon watches me. "What did she do?"

"Not everything is about my sister," I laugh.

"Then…what did *he* do?"

"Why do you think my mood is linked to another person?"

"Because I know you," he replies, scratching his neck.

"There's only two people who can rub you wrong. Adde and me. And since I'm out of the picture, I've come to the conclusion that Evander might have taken my spot."

He's not wrong.

While my sister is number one on my list of who can bring my blood to boil in seconds, he was a close second. But my brain has done an excellent job in masking that part of our relationship as I tried to wrap my head around what I could have done that he ended up leaving me.

"Was it ever your intention to marry me?" I ask, and my eyes widen when my own words register in my brain.

Leon seems to be taken aback by my question as much as I am. "One hundred percent."

"Then, explain to me: what made you leave?"

His breath comes out shallow as he contemplates his following words carefully. "Do you want the truth?"

"No, lie to me," I answer sarcastically to break the tension between us, but it doesn't work.

"I was scared you would eventually realize I'm just a normal guy."

"Nothing about you is normal," I laugh, shaking my head.

"That's where you're wrong. I can't give you a mansion, a fancy car, or even a nice vacation. I'm just a teacher who barely scrapes by."

Oh my freaking god! I had an entire year to break my head

about why Leon left, and money wasn't on my radar.

"That's what you think of me? That I'm superficial?"

He throws his hands in the air. "Look at your life. You own a bookstore chain and cabins on a mountain. Everything you touch turns into gold. There's nothing out there I can offer you, you can't get yourself."

That sounds vaguely familiar.

It's the same thought I had about Evander in the attic and again this morning when I compared my wishing power to his.

"It was never about money," I answer, shaking my head. "We could have lived in a cardboard box together, and I would have been happy as long as you were with me. That was all in your head."

"I realized that too," he says, taking a step in my direction. "But I was too ashamed to reach out to you. When River asked me to be his best man and told me you would be here, I knew this would be my chance to explain everything to you." He lowers his head. "But you moved on. I'm too late."

"You're not," I reply without thinking.

He cocks an eyebrow. "You're taken."

Oh shit. Yeah, there's that.

"It's not what it looks like. I'm—"

"Is everything alright out here?" Evander asks, leaning out the door.

And there he is—my fake boyfriend, aka cockblock.

Leon takes a step back to signal Evander that he's behaving. But I don't want him to. If I had known that my sister planned on housing Leon with me, I would have ripped her a new butthole, but I would have come anyway. I couldn't miss her big day just because my ex was there.

I never thought my feelings for him would rekindle as fast as they are now. I felt the desire to touch him in the hot tub, and he knows it as well as I do. If Evander hadn't interrupted, I can't say for sure how last night would have ended.

"I'll be inside in a minute," I say, biting my lip. Evander looks at me, his eyes forming into slits as he observes us. After a few moments, he closes the door to leave us alone.

"I don't know what to do," I say, studying Leon.

"There's nothing you *can* do," he says, grabbing his neck again. "All I wanted was to come clean and tell you I still love you. You deserve the truth."

I have no words.

"You can't just… it's not… it's not fair," I mumble, my breath ragged as I keep replaying his last two sentences in my head.

"I'm sorry," he says, returning slowly to the door. "Let's just get through the weekend, and you'll never see me again."

Flabbergasted, I stand there as Leon leaves me behind— again.

I don't feel the cold burning on my skin as anger rushes through me. This can't be happening. He can't just march back into my life, trying to pick up where we left off.

Still, I want it. I miss waking up beside him. I miss his warm touch and our brainless conversation. I miss the familiarity we shared.

I wouldn't have needed a fake boyfriend if he had reached out to me a day before I entered my grandma's house. All of this could have played out in our favor.

But he didn't.

Now, there's nothing I can do until this wedding is over because this weekend isn't about me.

TWELVE

The beams of car headlights punctuate the darkness outside the cabin, casting long shadows that dance across the wooden table.

"Atlas always comes just in time when the work is done," Aunt Margaret says as she stabs her fork into a juicy piece of meat.

"That's not true," I whisper, but my aunt's sensitive ears are trained to catch the quietest whisper if it involves drama.

"He purposely booked his tickets to arrive today," she counters, her eyes staring right into my soul as she takes an enormous chunk out of her meat without cutting it.

"Because Emily had her first recital last night, and he didn't want to miss it," I reply, holding her stare.

Aunt Margaret rolls her eyes. "She's three. They paid good money to watch her stumble over a stage."

Well, she got me there. I know little about children, but from all the videos Atlas sent me about her outstanding talent for ballet, I can't see it either.

"She's four. And it was important to him," Adde cuts in, slowly rising off her chair. "And they are here now, so please be nice, Auntie."

A few seconds later, the door jumps open, flooding the cabin with a burst of chilly air. A small family steps inside, their faces flushed from the cold. Among them is a little girl, her eyes wide with wonder as she takes in her surroundings.

Without hesitation, the little girl darts forward, her tiny feet padding across the floor towards me waiting eagerly. With a joyful squeal, she launches into my arms, and I'm just fast enough to drop my fork and spin around to wrap her in a tight hug.

Overcome with emotion, I let her down and kneel to meet Emily at eye level, my heart swelling with love. "Hello, cutie pie," I whisper. "I've missed you so much."

Emily giggles gleefully, her laughter filling the room like music. Stretching her hands towards me, she signals for me to pick her up, her eyes sparkling excitedly. "Auntie. Auntie. Did you see it? Did you see my…my…I forgot the name."

I smile at her. "Your recital?"

She nods vigorously as I put her on my lap. "Your daddy sent me videos. You were amazing!"

Her blond curls brush against my cheeks. "I can't wait to do it again."

She leans into me, and her weight against my chest feels comforting. A sense of pure bliss washes over me as I hold her. From all the people in the room, Emily picked me to greet first.

"She's grown so much," Atlas remarks, his voice filled with pride as he approaches, enveloping me in a warm hug. Emily giggles as she gets wedged between us. "It feels like just yesterday she was a baby."

"I can't believe she'll be five next month," I reply, squeezing her again. "Time flies faster when you get older."

"I can't believe you made it," Olivia says as she stops beside my brother and leans in closer. "I heard your plus-one made quite the entrance." Her eyes scan the table. "Where is he?"

I'm uncertain if Adde informed our brother about Evander or if Aunt Margaret took it upon herself to spread the news. Either way, I should have known.

"It's nice to finally meet you," Evander says as he comes up beside me, and Olivia's eyes widen.

"Holy shit, girl! Where did you find him?" she whispers into my ear, her eyes glued to Evander. "It should be illegal to look that good."

"I'm still here," Atlas says behind us, and I let out a loud laugh that shakes Emily.

"Nice to meet you, too. I'm Atlas, a.k.a. the baby brother. And that's my wife Olivia and our daughter Emily. Please excuse my wife's behavior. She hasn't left the house much in the last few weeks."

I open my mouth to ask what's going on. Olivia is a social butterfly, and everyone knows she can't survive a day without a playgroup, coffee meetup, or at least a walk around their neighborhood.

Before I can ask them what's going on, Evander takes the opportunity to speak. "It's fine," he laughs, swatting his hand. "I get comments like that a lot."

"You should," Olivia chimes in, practically eating Evander with her eyes.

I can't stop laughing.

There's no doubt in my mind that Atlas was made for Olivia and the other way around. They found each other in middle school, and just a few weeks after graduation, the news of Emily spread through the family. I can't imagine a world without Atlas and Olivia being together or an alternate reality where Olivia has a filter. She speaks whatever comes to her mind, and I love it. She practically said what I felt when I laid eyes on Evander.

"We're starving. Airplane food is just the worst," Atlas says, scanning the table for available seats. "Are you good holding her for a minute?"

"Take your time," I answer, pressing my cheek against Emily. "She's in good hands."

As Atlas and Olivia find their seats, Emily nestles contently in my arms, regaling me with tales of her first airplane ride. Her eyes sparkle with excitement at each word, and I listen intently, hanging on to every precious word. In moments like this one, I wish I wouldn't have the constant feeling of throwing myself into work and actually move closer to my brother. I could listen to Emily's words forever!

Suddenly, the sound of a fork clinking against a glass cuts through the air, drawing everyone's attention to the head of the table. My father rises from his chair, his expression a mixture of pride and emotion as he addresses the gathered guests.

"Friends and family," he begins, his voice thick and trembling slightly. "I want to thank each and every one of you for being here today to celebrate my daughter's wedding. It means the world to us to have so many amazing people supporting us on their special day."

He pauses for a few heartbeats.

I know where this is going.

As he continues, tears well up in his eyes, and my throat closes. "I wish Chloe could be here with us today," he adds, his voice choking with sadness as he turns to Adde. "She would have been so proud of the woman you have become, and I know she would have loved to see you walk down the aisle tomorrow."

My heart aches as I listen to my father's speech; the pain of my mother's absence is a constant ache in my soul. I hold Emily tighter, seeking comfort in the warmth of her embrace.

This is the part I've been dreading, but I thought my father would wait until tomorrow to speak of her. Mentally, I already planned to get wasted before the speeches even started. But now, I'm sober and choking on the bile rising in my throat.

As my father's speech goes on, I can feel the wave of sadness that threatens to drown me. The absence of my mother looms large over the festivities, a poignant reminder of the family member we lost—the lost love that scared me for life and made me promise never to love again.

Quietly, I rise from my seat, Emily still nestled in my arms. Silently, I reach my brother, gently transferring the half-sleeping child into his waiting arms. He gives me a knowing look, understanding the turmoil of emotions that churn within me.

"Thank you," Atlas whispers, his eyes as red as mine. "I'll see you later. Now get out of here."

With a heavy heart, I slip out of the cabin, the cool night air offering a welcome respite from the overwhelming emotions that threaten to consume me. I wander aimlessly through the darkness, seeking solace in the quiet solitude of the night.

As I walk, my thoughts turn to my mother; her presence feels keenly in the absence of her physical form. Memories flood my mind—the sound of her laughter, the warmth of her embrace, the gentle touch of her hand. Tears sting my eyes as I grapple with the pain of her loss, longing for just one more moment with the woman who shaped my life in countless ways.

In the night's stillness, I find myself drawn to a quiet corner of my cabin, a secluded spot in my library where I can be alone with my thoughts. I sink to the ground, my emotions overwhelming me as I dive into the darkness.

In just a few short months, I'll be older than my mother ever was. The thought of outliving her age hurts so freaking much.

Surrounded by thousands of words, I allow myself to grieve— for the mother I lost, for the pain of her absence, and the bittersweet moments of joy that will always be tinged with sadness.

And as I sit alone, surrounded by the echoes of her memories, I find a glimmer of hope amidst the pain; the knowledge that even in the darkest of times, her love will always be my guiding light.

THIRTEEN

The room floods with light as someone flicks on the overhead switch. Blinking against the sudden brightness, my vision slowly adjusts, revealing the familiar figure of Evander standing before me. His presence brings a sense of comfort, a glimmer of solace amidst the darkness.

His eyes wander to the open whiskey bottle beside me, his brow furrowing in concern as he approaches. "Hey," he breathes, his voice filled with gentle concern. "Are you okay? Do you want to talk about it?"

I shake my head, the weight of my pain too heavy to bear. I feel a lump rise in my throat, choking back the words that threaten to spill forth. Instead, I simply gesture for him to join me, my silent plea for companionship echoing in the quiet of the room.

With a nod, Evander settles down beside me, the warmth of his presence a comforting balm against the chill of the night. For a moment, we sit in silence; the only sound is the soft rustle of his breath as he watches me intently.

Sensing the need to lighten the mood and leave the pit of sadness I've been stuck in, I suggest playing a game—a distraction from the weight of my troubles. "Never have I ever," I say with a faint smile, my voice tinged with a hint of mischief. "Care to join me?"

Evander chuckles softly, a hint of amusement dancing in his eyes. "Sure, why not?" he replies.

I reach for the whiskey bottle and two glasses hidden behind some books beside me. I pour two generous glasses before placing them on the floor between us. With a trembling hand, I raise mine in a silent toast before taking a sip, the warm liquid burning a path down my throat.

"Never have I ever been in love," I say, my voice barely above a whisper. I glance at him, knowing full well his answer to my question.

He meets my gaze with a wistful smile, his eyes betraying a depth of emotion that mirrors mine. "Guilty as charged," he replies, his voice tinged with a hint of sadness.

I nod in understanding before taking a sip, my heart aching at the shared pain that binds us. For a moment, we sit in silence, lost in the memories of love lost and dreams left unfulfilled.

Then, it's Evander's turn to ask a question. "Never have I ever told someone about my heartache," he says, his eyes landing on my glass as he takes a sip out of his.

I don't pick up my glass because, as far as I can remember, I never told anyone about how I really feel about losing my mother. I had my chances, like the therapist who tried to lure my trauma out of me, or my brother, sister, and father, but I didn't take them because showing weakness isn't my thing.

Yet, my heart constricts at the raw vulnerability in his words. Evander told someone about his heartbreak, and I wish I were the one he said it to.

"Never have I ever met a djinn," I say with a smirk, and without hesitation, I lift my glass to my lips and take a long, slow sip. The bitter taste of whiskey lingers on my tongue.

"I'm not sure if I should drink or not," Evander laughs nervously.

"You should," I say, smirking at him, and I watch his lips curl around the thin glass as he does.

"Never have I ever wished for someone to wear a ducky float in a hot tub," he replies with a grin, and it takes me a moment to stop laughing to take a sip.

"Never have I ever taken a stranger to a family gathering," Evander says, and I almost spill my drink as I move my hand way too fast to stop him from completing his sentence.

"It's my turn," I giggle, shaking my head.

"Drink," he replies, pressing his lips together to hide his smile.

I rub my chin. "But not alone," I reply, trying to find

something I can use against him. "Never have I ever stalked a girl," I add, grinning at him.

"Stalking? I would call it *keeping an eye on her*, but I guess that's true," Evander replies, almost draining his entire glass.

He wipes his mouth before speaking. "Never have I—"

The front door rattles violently as someone bangs against it, interrupting our game.

"Don't open it," I say, pushing myself to my feet, but I lose my balance when I try to straighten up.

Evander grabs my arm and catches me before I can hit the ground. "Woah, slow down," he says, steadying me.

While sitting, I didn't realize how much the alcohol was affecting me already. Indeed, I could feel my head getting woozy, but I thought I still had everything under control.

"Stay here. Whoever it is, I'll turn them around." He lets me down gently, and my graceful attempt to pretend I'm okay fails when I lean back and hit my head on the shelf behind me.

His eyes linger on me. "I got this."

Every fiber of my body tells me to follow him, but my legs won't listen when I command them to move. Accepting the defeat, I strain my ears to hear who followed us.

Is it Leon again?

Probably.

Or it's my father to check on me.

It could also be Atlas, since he said he would come for me.

My sister's shrill voice fills the cabin as the door opens. "I need to take a shower."

"Use your own bathroom!" I yell, irritation bubbling up inside me.

I noticed her tousled hair and strands escaping from the confines of her usual carefully styled bun during the rehearsal dinner, but I thought nothing of it.

"I would, but we don't have warm water!" she yells back, and I don't have to be in the room to know that Adde is brushing past Evander, searching for me. "Please. I need to wash my hair," she exclaims, her voice urgent. "I can't go to bed with it like this. The hairstylist needs a good foundation to work with tomorrow."

"No problem," Evander replies, but I can hear my sister's frantic footsteps coming closer. "I'll take care of the cold water situation in your cabin's bathroom."

"I'll use your shower in the meantime," she replies, her voice coming closer and closer.

"That's not what I mean," Evander says, and the sound of a slamming door tells me she found the bathroom attached to the main living space and my bedroom.

Evander returns to me with a weary smile. "Looks like we've got a bit of a situation on our hands," he remarks, his eyes twinkling with amusement.

I groan, rubbing my temples as if trying to ward off an impending headache. "Tell me about it," I mutter, my voice tinged with exasperation. "She's always been like this–running around like a chicken with its head cut off, especially when it comes to wedding stuff."

I hear Adde turning on the water, since the bathroom is between the library and my room. I must be lucky and still have warm water because the squeaky noise of her feet dragging over the shower's ground comes through the wall.

As we wait for Adde to finish in the bathroom, another knock shakes the cabin.

"Really?" I whisper, biting my lip.

"Don't worry," Evander says, returning to the door.

"Is Adde here?" River asks, and I'm relieved it's him and not Leon.

"Let him in," I yell, knowing he won't leave without her.

"Bathroom," Evander says, and I hear a door open and shut before he returns to me.

"The pre-wedding chaos, the last-minute details, and the inevitable moments of panic and stress are getting to Adde," I say, rolling my eyes. "I promise you, she's usually not this bad."

"I find it quite entertaining," Evander replies. "Now, where were we?"

I look at my half-empty glass, and he follows my gaze. "Oh no. You're having water for the rest of the night," he says, smiling at me. I don't even react this time when I watch my whisky drain before being replaced with water.

I pull my lip up. "Not fair."

Evander raises his hands to signal he's innocent. "I don't make the rules." He approaches me with a mischievous glint in his eye. "So, shall we continue our game?" he asks, gesturing towards his glass.

I chuckle. "Sure, why not," I reply, my smile widening after I take a big gulp of water. "But this time, I'm going to make sure I win."

"We'll see."

FOURTEEN

I gesture to Evander to be silent when I hear a rhythmic banging behind me.

"What is it?" Evander asks after a few heartbeats.

I shrug my shoulders. "I don't know."

Is someone else knocking on my door?

"It comes from the bathroom," Evander says, pointing at the shelf behind me.

Heat rushes to my cheeks when another sound joins the thudding.

A moan.

Are they…

No, I must be hallucinating. My sister would never do that to me. Adde would never—

The thudding noise slows down, and I exhale sharply. There must be another explanation.

A muffled voice comes through the wall, and my cheeks heat

again when I hear my sister say: "Don't slow down."

Immediately, the thudding sound quickens, followed by a slapping noise of skin meeting skin.

Disgust rises into my throat…but with it arousal. The thudding slows down and picks up again, and all I can think of is my own desire, my pussy throbbing with need to be filled with a dick, hands grabbing my hips to thrust deeper into me.

No, this is wrong.

My eyes search the room, and I swallow hard when I see Evander's eyes on me. He looks at me like I'm prey. Or is it the other way around?

Do djinns have desires? In particular, sexual desires since that's all I can think of right now.

The knocking sounds intensify, and I have to press my legs together to stop my pussy from clenching as I think about someone taking me right here and right now.

"I'm sorry," I whisper, draining the glass of water before standing up on my wobbly feet.

Evander stares at me, and I hold a finger in the air to stop him in his tracks when he moves in my direction. If he comes any closer, I will throw myself around his neck.

Louder moans echo through the cabin as the slapping picks up, and I hear my soon-to-be brother-in-law grunts as he thrusts into my sister relentlessly.

Please make it stop. I can't take it any longer.

And then there's silence.

"I know a record when I hear one," Evander says, grinning at me, and I can't believe what he said.

Did he make a joke about their quickie? If I heard it right, that means he knows exactly what they were doing in there.

He studies me as I try to balance myself to show Evander that I'm fine and can care for myself. Somehow, I make it into the living room without bumping into a shelf or the doorframe, and I'm proud of myself.

When did I become such a lightweight?

Finally, after what feels like an eternity, the bathroom door swings open, and Adde emerges, her hair damp and freshly washed. She flashes a grateful smile at Evander before turning to me. "Thanks for letting me use your shower," she says with relief. "I feel so much better now."

I roll my eyes. "Just hurry and get out," I reply before telling her we heard everything.

Everything!

River follows her, his grin so vast that he keeps his head low to hide it.

"Any time," Evander replies as he closes the door behind them before spinning in my direction. I'm already half-way to my room when I feel his eyes on me. "What now?"

"We go to sleep," I answer, reaching for the door, but my perception is way off. It takes me another six steps until my fingers curl around the cold metal knob, and as if I'm being chased, I burst into my room before locking it from the inside.

The heat between my legs hasn't subsided. The sound of them having hot and steamy sex, just a thin wall away, rings in my ears. If Evander had made a wrong move, my intoxicated ass would have been determined to test how much a djinn knows about sex.

But I can't do that to him, nor myself.

I know how all of this would play out after I had him. The thrill of something new and exciting would wear off, either because I claimed my trophy or because I realized that my heart was getting involved, and that's never a good thing.

I'm a strong, independent woman who doesn't need a man— or djinn, for that matter.

I guess that is a lie, since Evander has been helping me for years now. That's another reason I can't make a move.

I fish my phone out of my pocket and turn on the flashlight. My eyes land on my suitcase, and I grin when I realize I packed it when I thought I was traveling alone to my cabin. I double-check that the door is locked, and I stumble to the suitcase on the ground beside my bed on wobbly feet. It only takes me a few seconds to find what I'm searching for, and the heat in my core stirs as my eyes land on the pink, velvety silicone vibrator and its remote.

I remember the exact book I read when I decided I needed

this wearable toy. The thought of reading the smutty pages of a book while pleasuring myself without using my hands—I need those to hold the book—pops back into my head.

It was the best decision I ever made.

After kicking my shoes off, I crawl into bed and turn on the small night light on the nightstand.

I should wait a few minutes to ensure that Evander is asleep, and the air is clear, but I can't. Just the touch of the soft material sends a hot pulse to my vagina. It's like she knows what I'm holding in my hand and can't wait for it.

My desire wins, like always.

After covering myself with two layers of blankets to dampen the sound of the vibration, I press the vibrator's button and lean down to insert it. I drag the toy through my folds, coating it with slick moisture as I tease it back and forth. After a few gentle pushes, it smoothly slips into place, stretching my vagina.

It feels so fucking good.

I position the smaller curved part against my clit and spread my legs wide before I turn the remote on.

Nine choices.

There are nine different vibration modes I can choose from, and I know every single one by heart. Out of those nine, I have two favorites: the steady on-and-off vibrations that mimic a dick going in-and-out, and the escalator—the vibration intensifies with each vibration until it starts from the beginning.

My vagina is set on imitating the thuds that brought me into this predicament.

I hit the mode button, and my body clenches as the first violent vibration courses through my clit, fueling the throbbing need of my lust. I press it twice until I reach my desired mode and put the remote on the blanket as my back arches with the twitching smooth material inside me. Each pulse makes my body tremble, and I press my hand to my mouth as an unexpected moan escapes my mouth. I can feel the heat building up in my lower belly as I move against the quivering toy.

Closing my eyes, I imagine a faceless man standing before me, spreading my legs wide before thrusting into me. I imagine his dick inside me, going in and out with the throbbing toy and envisioning his hand rubbing my clit while he bites into my neck.

Without having a say, my mind throws the image of Evander's cock at me. I can almost feel the way his dick hardens into steel, his rigid length right before me, begging me to touch him. We're in the hot tub again, and I reach out, my hand stretching around his girth as I squeeze him.

My breathing becomes ragged as I move my hips against the image in my vision, and when I hear a loud thud outside my dream, I rip my eyes open, and a shudder runs down my spine when I see Evander standing in the bathroom door.

"Is everything alright?" he asks, scanning the room, and I press my legs shut and pull violently on my blankets to cover as much of my body as I can even though I'm fully clothed, waist up. The tug on the blankets is strong enough to send the remote flying through the room, and panic grips me as I follow its fall to the ground close to the other door.

Another shudder runs through me as the vibration keeps its steady rhythm, and my vagina clenches around the vibrator like a lifeline.

This can't be happening. Why didn't I think of the bathroom door?

My first instinct is to pull the vibrator out, but without my pussy dampening the sound, Evander will hear the vibration before I can turn it off manually.

"I'm fine," I answer, the last word coming out in a hushed moan as my body reacts to the stimulation from within.

"Do you need that?" Evander asks, stepping into the room to reach for the remote.

Please, no. Don't pick it up. Leave it there. Don't—

My eyes widen when he picks up the device and my imagination goes through the roof when I see how small it looks compared to his big hand.

At this point, my clit is so sensitive, each vibration sends a tremble through my body, and I need to press my lips together to muffle a moan as Evander's finger finds the mode button and hits it.

"What is this?" he asks, turning the remote in his hands, and

I buck against the new mode that hits my pussy and clit like a tidal wave.

The thought of him being in control of my pleasure sends wild images through my head.

"Just throw it to me and leave," I croak, stretching my trembling hand toward him.

"What's the magic word?"

"Please," I add, feeling the warmth in my lower belly building.

Evander's eyes land on me as he walks over to me. "That's better."

"Throw it!" I plead, using every ounce of self-control I have left to stop myself from showing signs of what's happening beneath the blankets.

"Are you sure you're alright? Your cheeks are glowing," he replies, coming to a halt beside the bed, and I can feel the sweat forming on my skin as I fight my arousal with every fiber of my body.

"Go," I pant as another wave of pleasure rushes through my clit into my lower abdomen.

Evander's gaze wanders over the blankets covering me until his eyes lock with mine again. They turn into slits as a viscous smile curls his lips, and before I can move, he picks up the remote and presses the button again.

For fuck's sake.

My body shakes as my vibrator switches modes, hitting my G-spot and clit with its strongest setting. Involuntarily, my legs spread with the pleasure pulsating inside me, and my hips buck against the device.

Evander's grin widens as he repeatedly presses down on the remote, zipping through the modes like a flickering lightbulb. My pussy clenches around the vibrator as the different modes hit me with an unsteady beat, and I press my mouth shut to at least stop myself from moaning right in front of him.

"Does it feel good?" Evander asks, finally pausing on a mode.

"I don't know…what… you're talking about," I pant.

The initial wave of embarrassment subsides when I see the darkness in his eyes—his desire. His gaze roams over me, indicating that he knows precisely what is going on between my legs.

My eyes land on his waistline and slowly move lower as I move to the rhythm he gives me through the remote in his hand. There, strained against his pants, is the dick he almost pressed into my face last night as he stepped into the tub. I can see its massive outline, the tip pressing against the fabric in my direction.

"Wish for it, Darling," he growls through gritted teeth as he massages the remote in his hands.

"I wish—"

My orgasm slams so hard into me as I envision his dick lining up with my entrance. Shudder after shudder overwhelms my body as my pussy grips the vibrator again and again until, finally, my body stops shaking.

What follows is pure overstimulation as the vibration keeps moving my swollen clit, and I act fast to pull it out, leaving it to shake the mattress beneath me.

The heat that was flowing through my veins and pussy redirects and streams right to my face as I see Evander taking me in.

I'm a hot mess.

"Sweet dreams," he says, pressing the power button, and the bed stops shaking.

"I wish for snow," I say, closing my eyes as if, by looking at him, I risk the magic not to work. But also because I started a stupid wish and can feel its demand to be finished.

Really, after everything that just happened, all I can think of is freaking snow?

Evander walks to the door and looks over his shoulder. "Nice safe," he says as he closes the door behind him, leaving me alone with my crippling anxiety.

FIFTEEN

Before I even open my eyes, I can feel the burning embarrassment from last night slam into me.

He made me come without ever touching me.

How can I look him in his eyes now? Even worse, how can I survive today while Evander and Leon are here?

Maybe it was a dream? It could be, right? Perhaps this was just a wild fantasy I had after all the whisky.

I exhale with a pounding headache, the remnants of last night's revelry still echoing in my mind. Groaning, I rub my temples and slowly push myself upright in bed. As I blink blearily at the morning light filtering through the cabin window, a pang of anxiety shoots through me.

I stumble out of bed, my limbs heavy with exhaustion and regret. The memories of the previous night come flooding back in full force—the laughter, the sadness, the endless stream of drinks. But amidst the haze of alcohol, one thing stands out—I need to face Evander sooner or later and tell him I wasn't myself last night.

Heart pounding, I march into the cabin's main room, my eyes scanning the empty space for any sign of him. But he's nowhere to be found.

Frantically, I search the library, the bathroom, even the closet, but he's gone, and there is no trace of his presence.

Panic grips my chest as I realize I'm alone. My heart pounds in my ears as memories of Leon's abrupt departure flood my mind. The same sinking feeling washed over me just months ago, a sense of déjà vu threatening to drown me.

This can't be happening to me again. Evander can't just leave me.

But…what if he never existed? What if I imagined all of this? What if I started drinking before I set foot on that plane, painting the picture of finding a djinn to ease my mind?

I don't know what's real anymore.

With a trembling hand, I reach for my phone, my fingers shaking as I dial my brother's number. He's the only one I trust right now. Even though he's only a cabin away, I don't have the patience to wait for an answer. He would tell me if Evander was just an elaborate figment of my wild imagination.

But there is no answer, just the hollow echo of silence on the other end of the line. Tears sting my eyes as I realize he's truly gone, leaving me all alone once again—if he was even real to begin with.

A guttural scream tears from my throat, the sound echoing off the walls of the empty cabin. I sink to my knees, the weight of my despair pressing down on me like a crushing weight.

But even as my heart breaks, I know I can't afford to wallow in self-pity.

With a deep breath, I push myself upright, wiping away the tears that stain my cheeks.

I can't let myself fall apart, not now. There's too much at stake—my sister's wedding, my role as the maid of honor. I have to be strong for my family and myself because I've done it once, and I'll do it again.

Determined to push through the pain, I make my way to the bathroom, the hot water of the shower offering a brief respite from the storm raging inside me. As the steam fills the room, I close my eyes, letting the warmth seep into my bones, easing the ache of my heart.

Once I'm clean and dressed in the comfortable pajamas Adde gave me, I gather my strength to get through this day and set out into the biting cold of the morning. The snow is fresh and deep, the air crisp and unforgiving, but I trudge on, my footsteps steady despite my utter disappointment.

Finally, I reach the small cabin beside mine, my sister's home for the duration of the wedding festivities. With a heavy heart and a forced smile, I knock on the door, steeling myself for the next hours ahead.

Adde greets me with a warm hug and a knowing look, her eyes filled with empathy. "I'm sorry," she whispers, her voice soft with understanding. "I know how hard this must be for you."

How does she already know? And what exactly is she referring to? Does she know I made up a man because I was so desperate to please my family, or did Evander really exist, and he said his goodbyes to my family before leaving?

"It must be hard to be included in a wedding so close to your original date. I knew it was too much to invite Leon, but River insisted on it. If you have second thoughts, please let me know, and I'll cut him from the ceremony."

I nod, my throat tight with emotion. "I'll be okay," I reply, my voice wavering slightly. "Seriously though, I'm so happy for you."

How could I forget about my own wedding? Perhaps because I burned the printed invitations alongside the calendar that marked the *happiest day in my life* just days after I realized Leon wouldn't return.

It didn't even cross my mind that I'd see Leon at the end of the aisle. And to make matters worse, isn't the maid-of-honor and best man supposed to walk down the aisle together, arm in arm?

Fuck! Can this day get any worse?

We sit down, side by side, on wooden chairs, bathed in the

soft glow of the cabin's morning light. Before us, a stylist works diligently, curling our hair and expertly applying makeup to prepare for the wedding.

Radiant with excitement, Adde recounts how she met her fiancé—a casual encounter at a coffee shop that blossomed into a whirlwind romance. Her eyes sparkle with joy as she speaks, her voice filled with love and affection for the man who captured her heart.

"I'm telling you, it was love at first sight," Adde laughs, throwing her head back.

"No, it wasn't," I answer, smirking at her. "You met him before and didn't notice him."

"That doesn't count. We were kids when we met. I'm talking about when I saw him ordering a double espresso to go with his chocolate croissant."

"I'm happy for you," I repeat, and I mean it.

As I listen to her go on about their first date, a story I've heard a million times, a smile plays at the corners of my lips as I watch my sister's happiness unfold. But I can't help but feel a twinge of envy as she talks about her future—the plans for a family, the dreams of babies, and maybe even a dog. It was everything I swore I never wanted for myself, but somehow, it feels wrong.

I always imagined settling down and building a life with someone I love. But as I look at myself in the mirror, I see no fiancé by my side, no plans for the future, just the empty ache of loneliness that seems to grow with each passing day. That part of me that had the longing for love died a long time ago before Leon showed me it could be possible before stomping on that dream again.

As I stare at myself, I see my mother: the reason I am the way I am.

The thought of creating something so fragile, a family that can be taken from you at any moment without notice, is the scariest thing on the planet.

For a moment, I allow myself to run through the worst-case scenarios of having a family, the weight of my unfulfilled dreams I had as a child pressing down on me like a suffocating blanket.

But then I force myself to push aside my insecurities and focus on the task at hand. Today is about celebrating my sister's happiness, not dwelling on my shortcomings. I try to bury the ache in my chest, to push aside the nagging voice in my head that whispers of unfulfilled dreams and lost opportunities.

No, I made my choice, and once I'm back home, I'll feel better.

"Evander is an early riser," Adde says, her eyes closed as she gets her light eyeshadow applied.

My body stiffens. "What did you say?"

"Evander. He was up pretty early this morning."

My heart jumps into my throat. "You saw him?"

"At five I couldn't sleep anymore, so I got some food to calm my stomach. He scared the living hell out of me when I found him in the kitchen," she says casually.

Adde saw him.

"We talked for a minute, but he seemed to be in a rush," she adds.

Yeah, to get the hell away from me.

"Are you sure Leon can stay?" she asks, changing the subject. "I don't want to be responsible for breaking you two up. He speaks highly of you, plus I haven't seen you this happy since…you know…Leon."

My mind races as my heart splits. If Adde saw Evander this morning, where is he now? Why didn't he come back? And why can't I tell her I don't want to be paired up with Leon? Do I still have feelings for him, or is it the familiarity I crave?

"Evander can be restless," I say as nonchalantly as possible. "And don't worry about Leon. We talked, and I got the clarity I needed to end that chapter of my life."

This lie better not bite me in the ass later. I mean, we talked, and he told me why he left, but all it did was open up old wounds I thought healed.

"I should check on Evander," I say, looking at my reflection again.

Adde swats her hand at me without moving her face. "He's with the boys. He's fine," she replies. "I should have mentioned the change in plans. River thought it was a good idea to include

Evander as a groomsman."

I gasp.

Adde opens her eyes and sits up straighter. "I know. We should have consulted you before, but it was a last-minute decision. We can…"

I don't hear the rest my sister has to say because I am too busy trying to comprehend how I will get through today. Not only will I see my ex standing at the end of the aisle, but I'm also walking it down with my arm curled around a man who shouldn't exist in the real world and who made me orgasm with my vibrator.

This could all end now.

I could tell Adde that Evander isn't my partner and that I don't know how I feel about facing Leon during the ceremony, but the pleading glint in her eyes for approval forces me to say the words she wants to hear.

"Thank you so much for including him."

The smile crossing Adde's face tells me she's relieved. Good for her because my anxiety just reached a level I didn't know existed.

SIXTEEN

I pace through the largest cabin, my heart pounding with anticipation as I survey it. Everything looks perfect—the tables are elegantly set and decorated, the flowers are arranged in delicate bouquets, and the soft glow of candlelight bathes the room in a warm, inviting ambiance.

But as I approach the floral arrangements, my heart skips a beat. The roses, which I accidentally ordered in pristine white, have inexplicably turned a deep shade of red.

He kept his word.

Marveling at the white and red decor, I turn around, and my eyes meet those of a man standing before me, his sun-kissed skin glowing in the soft light of the venue. He's dressed in a burgundy suit that looks so different from the usual green or beige I have seen him in before.

For a moment, I'm speechless, and before I can speak, he steps forward, a warm smile playing at the corners of his lips.

"You look breathtaking," he says softly, his voice filled with sincerity.

Heat floods my cheeks at the compliment, my heart fluttering in my chest. But as quickly as the warmth spread through me, a surge of resentment rises within me.

"Why did you have to scare me like that?" I demand, my voice tinged with frustration. "I thought you had left."

His smile falters, replaced by a look of remorse. "I'm sorry," he replies earnestly, his brown eyes filled with regret. "I didn't intend to worry you."

Despite my lingering annoyance, the sincerity in his voice softens my heart. I sigh, willing to let go of my frustration and focus on the present moment.

It isn't his fault that I have separation anxiety.

Just as my body relaxes, the image of his hand curled around the remote jumps to the front of my mind. Immediately, warmth creeps into my face.

"It's okay," I reply, my tone getting softer. "About yesterday. I need you to know that the version you saw of me wasn't me. I…"

As I speak, Evander reaches into his pocket, pulling out a small box and holding it out to me. "I thought it would be nice to have this," he says, taking a step back to give me space.

My eyes widen in surprise as I accept it, thankful for his ignorance about last night. I was prepared for the worst, but here we are, and he's acting like it never happened.

My fingers tremble slightly as I lift the lid. Inside, nestled among delicate tissue paper, is a small, sparkly keychain. As I lift it out of the box, I see a photo of my mother smiling back at me from behind the glass.

Tears prick at my eyes as I realize the significance of the gift.

"Attach it to your flowers," Evander says softly, his voice filled with tenderness. "So she can be with you on this special day."

With trembling hands, I turn to Evander. "Why are you doing this to me?" I ask, my voice barely above a whisper.

The smile vanishes off his face. "Do you remember you owe me wishes?"

Is he kidding me? He's demanding one of his wishes now, right after he hands me a physical reminder of my mother.

"I wish to know what happened to her," he says, his demand pressing the air out of my lungs.

I shake my head. "I can't do this," I reply, putting the keychain back into the box and closing it. "Not here, not now."

"It has been almost twenty years, Carena. There's never the perfect moment to talk about a deep loss."

Nausea creeps up my throat as I study him. "Why? From all the wishes you could have picked from, why do you want to know about *her*?"

"Because I can't help you if I don't know what's going on in your head."

Every emotion known to humankind rushes through me as I digest his words.

"I don't need a knight in shining armor. You have no right to ask me that question. I barely know you."

"Then let's change that."

"I don't want to," I say, holding the box in his direction. "Bringing you here was a mistake."

He tilts his head. "Because I asked about your mother?"

"No, because I was doing just fine before you appeared in my life," I huff, my body trembling.

"You can't keep lying to yourself."

"I'm not, and I don't need to explain myself. This arrangement we have is over."

When I realize he won't take the box from me, I let go of it. My heart shatters when it hits the ground, and every fiber of my body tells me to bend down and pick it back up, but my anger is more potent.

"I release you from our agreement," I hiss through clenched teeth.

Evander chuckles. He fucking chuckles!

"I can't leave before the scales are even," he says, and the rage burning inside me brings tears to my eyes.

"What does that mean?"

"Until you haven't granted my wishes, I won't be able to

leave."

Is that the real reason he stayed? Was it his intention to bind me to him through wishes?

"Well, you better hope I don't live forever, because what you're asking is none of your business." I storm past him and come to a screeching halt as he appears before me. "I wish I never met you," I say, my hands curling into fists.

He blinks at me, and I expect him to vaporize, but when he's still there a few heartbeats later, I groan. "Stop blocking my wishes."

"It's not me."

"Then whose fault is it?"

Evander just stares at me. "What happened to her, Carena?"

Why is he doing this to me?

No matter what I do next, Evander has all the time in the world to haunt me. When I accepted his deal, I never imagined his wish would demand to open up a trauma I'm not ready to talk about.

But how long can I fight him? He's not asking for much. A sentence would be enough to get me out of this predicament until he demands his next wish.

"My mother died when I was ten years old," I begin, clenching my teeth. "She had a brain aneurysm in her sleep and never woke up."

Despite the passage of time, the pain of her loss still lingers, a constant ache in my heart.

"She was the most wonderful person," I continue, recalling her beautiful face. "Kind, loving, and full of life."

Tears well up in my eyes as I speak, the weight of her grief pressing down on me like a heavy burden. But even as the tears spill down my cheeks, I feel a sense of relief wash over me, releasing the pent-up emotions that have been building inside me for so long.

Evander reaches for me, and I want to pull back, but I'm frozen in place as he squeezes my hand gently, offering me silent reassurance and support. "What happened after her death?"

I shrug my shoulders. "Nothing. Life went on as normal."

Why can't I breathe? Why does it feel like my heart is trying to claw its way out of my chest, leaving my rare soul wide open for Evander to see?

He tilts his head. "What happened, Carena?"

The instinct to run flashes inside my head like a blinking warning sign, yet when I look into his eyes, I can see the hurt he's experiencing as he watches my struggle to fulfill his wish.

"I was the oldest. I had to take care of my father and siblings."

"So, at ten, you jumped in for your mother?"

"What else was I supposed to do?" I shake my head. "I answered your question, and now state your next wishes so I can be done with you."

His chest moves slowly up and down. "It's not the right time."

What does he mean by *it's not the right time*?

Knowing I owe someone a wish with no time limit, which could be anything, is maddening. Is he doing this to me because I used his powers without ever considering how it feels? Is this his way of showing me how terrible it is to be in someone's debt?

"You better come up with it quickly," I say, pushing him out of the way.

SEVENTEEN

I stand beside Adde, my hand resting gently on her shoulder as we wait in the cabin. I'm unsure where Evander went after I stormed back into my cabin to catch my breath.

Why do I keep doing this to him? I've never met someone who went under my skin so deeply—yet my heart longs for his nearness.

I should have asked him how his morning went. He was stuck in my brother's cabin, not only with Atlas, but also with River and Leon, as they got ready for the ceremony.

The thought of Evander and Leon in one room— undressing—sends a flash of heat into my lower belly.

I close my eyes and shake my head to scramble that image.

That fantasy of yours will never happen, Carena.

When I open them again, the air is charged with nervous energy, the soft strains of music drifting into my ears as the moment I've been dreading draws closer.

Adde fidgets nervously before me, her eyes darting around the room as if searching for an escape. "I'm about to throw up," she admits, her voice trembling slightly. "What if I trip or mess up my vows? What if he doesn't show up?"

I smile reassuringly, squeezing her shoulder. "You're going to be fine," I breathe. "This is what you've been dreaming of—the chance to marry the love of your life surrounded by friends and family who love and support you."

But my sister's nerves only seem to grow, her anxiety mounting with each passing moment. "And what about the snow?" she adds, gesturing towards the window where a heavy blanket of white covers the ground outside. "I wanted a winter wedding, but I didn't expect it to snow this much. What if it ruins everything?"

I glance out the window, taking in the sight of the snow-covered landscape.

This is all my fault. I wished for snow but didn't think Evander would let it get this far.

"It's beautiful," I say softly to ease her mind. "And besides, a little snow can't ruin your special day. If anything, it adds to the magic of the moment."

As we speak, the soft strains of music grow louder, signaling the start of my entrance. I give Adde's hand one last reassuring squeeze before stepping back to give her space.

"I can't wait to see you walk down the aisle," I say, tears dwelling in my eyes.

With a deep breath, Adde squares her shoulders, her gaze fixed on the door ahead. "I love you," she whispers, her voice barely audible above the music.

My heart almost jumps out of my chest as I soak up her words. I can't remember the last time Adde said them to me. In all the years I took care of her, supported her, and cheered for her, she never thanked me once or showed affection.

"I love you, too," I whisper, and with that, I step through the door and out into the snow beyond, where Evander waits for me, his eyes searching for mine.

I can't look at him. Not after what he did to me and the way I reacted. Moments ago, I thought I was in the wrong, but when I see his neatly trimmed beard and wind-tousled hair, the memory of the bouquet jewelry pops back into my head.

"You have to make it stop," I whisper as we descend the snow-plowed path.

He grips my arm.

"Wish for it, Darling," he replies without looking at me.

"Are you mad? My last and only wish will be to get rid of you," I growl in a low tone so no one can hear me. "If you want to do the right thing, make it stop, or I'll force you."

He squeezes my arm tighter. "Are you threatening me?"

I look over at him, plastering a fake smile on my face. "Don't flatter yourself. It's just a warning."

"I like it when you get feisty. Your eyes show the same fire you had last night when you wanted me," he says, and my body stiffens at his words.

What the hell is happening?

I'm a hair's breadth away from slapping him on the cheek and storming down the aisle alone, but my eyes land on a sight that forces bile up my throat.

My gaze flickers briefly to the groom, but then my attention is drawn to the man beside him. At the end of the path stands Leon, a burgundy suit straining against his muscular arms and a grin on his face as our eyes lock.

This is how I imagined it.

No, wrong.

Even though I wear a faux fur coat, the cold biting my skin through the thin maroon-colored dress wasn't in my imagination as I dreamed of my wedding. I saw a blue sky, heard waves, and felt warmth beneath my bare feet as I looked into Leon's eyes.

But this is not my wedding and not my fiancé.

"You owe me," Evander whispers as we pass the first row of two rose-covered benches filled with guests.

I'm unsure if I can successfully mask my anger with a smile. I've practiced this smile in the mirror a million times while Adde got her hair done, and it doesn't feel the same.

I want to run.

With each step I get closer to Leon, the small path between dream and reality seems to thin. This could have been us if he hadn't walked out on me. Everything I ever wanted stands at the end of this aisle, yet it's out of reach.

I glance around at the benches and roses lining the path to distract myself. Were those flowers really worth it? I'm the only one who knows how much the roses are actually worth—a wish that will cost me more than I can imagine.

Beside me, Evander keeps a firm grip on my arm, guiding me forward with gentle reassurance. As we reach the makeshift altar, he lets go of me, allowing me to step forward independently. I move to the left, taking my place as the maid of honor, my eyes fixed on my ex-fiancé, who stands across from me as the best man. Our eyes meet briefly, but before I can dwell on our past any longer, the music changes, signaling the start of the bride's entrance.

I turn to the aisle once more, my heart skipping a beat as I watch Adde make her way toward us.

My sister looks stunning in the white dress, her dark wavy hair cascading down her shoulders in loose waves. A faux fur stole drapes elegantly around her shoulders, adding a touch of glamor to her winter wedding ensemble.

She was right. The red rose bouquet in her hands looks fantastic compared to the snow.

Tears well up in our father's eyes as he walks beside her, his hand gripping hers tightly as if reluctant to let her go. He kisses her cheek tenderly before taking his seat, his gaze filled with pride and love.

Adde reaches the altar, her hands trembling slightly as she clutches the bouquet. She looks radiant, her eyes shining with a mixture of nerves and excitement as she stops before me.

I reach out to take Adde's hand, offering her a reassuring smile. "You're doing the right thing," I whisper.

She returns my smile, her nerves melting away. "Thank you," she replies softly, her voice barely above a whisper as she pulls away from me.

My heart rate quickens when River takes her hand, his eyes shining with love and devotion. And as I stand beside Adde, watching her exchange vows with the man she loves, I feel the eyes of Leon and Evander burning into me.

I might be focused on the most important day of my sister's life, but they are not.

EIGHTEEN

There aren't many hiding places when you're stuck with over thirty people in a cabin, especially when the tables are pushed to the side to make room for a dance floor.

I've spent the entire evening trying to dodge Leon and Evander, their presence casting a shadow over what is supposed to be a joyous occasion.

As I put down my fourth champagne flute on the table, I can't help but feel a pang of sadness wash over me. The memories of my own failed engagement still linger in the air, which means I still haven't had enough alcohol to drown those damn feelings.

I need more booze.

"Friends and family," my father's voice booms through the cabin. "May I introduce to you, Mr. and Mrs. Engel."

The murmurs around me die as Adde and River step onto the dance floor as a married couple for the first time. I push aside my thoughts and turn my attention to them taking the center stage, their eyes locked in a tender embrace as they sway to the music.

Seeing them together fills me with a bittersweet mixture of joy and longing. I watch as they move gracefully across the dance floor, their love radiating from every step they take.

But as the song draws to a close, River breaks away from his bride and walks towards me. His eyes meet mine with a softness he usually only gives my sister, his hand outstretched in a silent invitation.

"May I have this dance?" he asks.

I look around.

He can't mean it. I'm Adde's sister and not...

"I can't," I whisper, shaking my head. "Pick someone else."

Not only am I four glasses deep already, but he can't expect me to replace my mother. If she had been here, it would have been her turn to dance with her new son-in-law.

But she's not...and I'm not her.

"Please," he whispers, his warm fingers touching mine. "You're the closest thing your sister has to a mother. It would mean the world to her to repay you for everything you've done for her."

My throat is so tight. I can't speak.

It doesn't sound like her, and yet, how else should River know what part I played in her childhood if it wasn't for her?

My heart skips a beat as I nod slowly, a small smile playing at the corners of my lips to cover the pain shooting through my chest.

We go to the dance floor together to join Adde and our father.

I glance up at River. "Congratulations," I say, trying to concentrate on my feet so I won't step on his toes. "You two were made for each other."

River smiles down at me, his man-bun slowly losing momentum as strands start to fall into his face. "Thank you," he replies softly, his hand tightening around mine in a silent gesture of support. "I wish I had more time to get to know you, but you're a very busy woman and hard to get a hold of."

If those words had crossed my sister's lips, I would immediately recognize them for the stab they were meant to be. But River really means it when I see the sadness crossing his features for a split second.

"I'll do better," I reply, trying to sound as convincing as possible.

As the music plays on, I allow myself to get lost in the moment, the worries and cares of the world slipping away as I dance with the man who is now a brother of mine.

Whatever compassion Adde is missing, River has enough for both of them. River twirls me around the dance floor, and I can't help but steal glances at Evander, who stands patiently at the edge, waiting for his turn to dance with me. His steadfast and unwavering presence fills me with another wave of rage—though dampened a little by the champagne.

Just as the groom leads us toward Evander, I make a split-second decision and subtly redirect our path away from him. I can't bear the thought of dancing with anyone else, even though Evander must have been waiting for me all night.

As the dance comes to an end, I prepare to walk away, my heart heavy with conflicting emotions. I've done everything Adde asked of me. Besides the bouquet toss, I made it through everything. Adde will understand if I'm not in line to catch the flowers I worked so hard to get.

But before I can make my escape, a hand suddenly grabs mine, pulling me into another dance.

My eyes widen when I look into Leon's blue eyes.

The familiar sensation of being in his arms is like muscle memory, the memories of our past swirling around us as we move across the dance floor. His touch is electric, sending shivers down my spine.

"We can still have this," he whispers, his voice filled with longing. "We can still be together. All you have to do is say the word."

My heart aches, torn between the desire to believe him and the knowledge that I can never forgive him for leaving me during our engagement. The wounds he inflicted run deep, leaving scars that will never fully heal.

He left me. *Me*!

What guarantee do I have that he won't walk out on me again?

Can I trust him? Can I say full-heartedly that he will be there every day, every morning, if I give him another chance?

Before I can respond, he tightens his grip on me, his desperation clear in his eyes.

"Let go of me," I wince as his nails dig into my skin.

Finally, I jerk away from him, my resolve hardening with each step I move out of his reach. "I can't."

My body shakes violently as I see the man I was about to marry for the first time. His bright blue eyes show no love as he reaches for me again. His blonde hair is styled back, strict, and unmoving. My eyes land on his neck, where large veins showcase the amount of restraint it takes him to not pounce on me.

"I can't forgive what you did," I growl, my chest heaving.

His face falls, a mask of hurt and disappointment as he realizes what I mean. The threat I saw in his eyes just moments ago vanishes.

That's the Leon I remember—controlled, sweet, and understanding.

How did I not see his wicked side? How could I have been so blind?

"You can't replace me like that," Leon replies, anger flashing back into his eyes. "Eventually, he will leave you, and you'll come crawling back."

"That's not fair," I whisper, fighting back the feeling of not being enough.

How dare he use my biggest fear against me? When he left me, he knew exactly how deep my fear of abandonment runs. He knew how much the death of my mother messed with me, and yet he abused that knowledge.

I had the tiniest glimmer of hope that he did it unconsciously, but now that I've seen the *real* Leon, I'm aware it was a calculated move.

As I open my mouth to unleash all my rage, a man steps forward, his broad chest blocking my ex-fiancé from view.

"Leave her alone," Evander says firmly, pushing me behind him.

My heart skips a beat as I look up at Evander's dark features. His eyes are warm and reassuring in my direction, filled with a sense of kindness and understanding I've never experienced before, but cold when he faces Leon again. He takes my hand in his, pulling me close as we begin to dance together.

After a few steps, a sense of peace washes over me, a feeling of safety and security in his arms. This stuff only happens in books and movies, yet here I am, pressed against Evander's chest as he sweeps me away from the man I once knew.

"Did he hurt you?" Evander asks, worry clouding his eyes.

I throw my head back and laugh, unsure if it's a genuine reaction or my way of covering up the pain I feel in my soul. "Do I look like a delicate flower to you?"

"I'm not talking about physical pain," he replies, searching my eyes, and I can feel an invisible hand caress my face.

"I'm alright," I respond, staring up at him.

Evander smiles at me. "Then, I guess, it's time for my second wish."

I cough. "Excuse me?"

Can I please catch a fucking break?

I was ready to forgive him for asking about my mother since he stopped Leon from making a scene.

Can't he read the room? Can't he see that I'm overwhelmed with everything that happened today?

"I wish to know how you're currently feeling," he says, pressing me against him.

With the next step, he spins me around before he pulls me back in. "That's not a wish," I answer, rolling my eyes.

"It is to me," he replies, smiling down at me.

I open my mouth and close it again.

Is he serious? Asking for my well-being isn't worth a wish.

Perhaps he finally came to the conclusion that he's not getting anywhere with me and decided to get those wishes out of the way so I could free him.

I don't blame him.

"I already told you. I'm fine."

His eyes twinkle at me. "I'll need a bit more than that."

What am I supposed to say?

"Getting through this day was harder than expected,

especially since I had to walk down the aisle staring at the man I once wanted to marry, and he turned out to be an ass."

Evander twirls me. "And?"

"I don't know what else you want from me."

"Reach deep. What do you feel?"

I close my eyes.

Emptiness.

A missing heart.

Anger.

Betrayal.

The tiniest sliver of hope.

"Nothing," I answer, looking up at him.

Evander grins, pressing his hand against my back. "It's still not enough."

Involuntarily, I arch my back, pressing my body against his. "Alright then. I'm sad. I wish I weren't drowning myself in work, overworking myself, so I don't have to return to an empty home. I wish I could find someone who loves me as unconditionally as my mother loved me. I wish my mother was here." I exhale. "But you already know all those wishes because I've told you those before, and you never granted a single one of them."

The warmth of his touch seeps through my thin dress and into my spine. "Perhaps it's the way you phrase your wishes. What can you do to change them since you already know that the way they are now goes against my rules?"

What does he want me to do? Rephrase them? Is this how it works?

Have I been asking for help the wrong way?

"I wish there was somebody at home worth returning to," I whisper, imagining what it would feel like not to be alone. I envision stepping through the door into a steady light greeting me instead of darkness. As I step in, I can feel the presence of another person waiting behind the next door.

"And I wish I could see my mother again."

Evander tilts his head, contemplating my wishes. "You know, I can't—"

My shoulders slump. "Bring back the dead? I know. It was still worth a shot."

He presses me tighter against him, and I can feel his breath caressing my face. "And your other wish is totally up to you. You'll never find someone if you keep running in your little hamster wheel until you tip over and die."

I want to lean away from him, but my body longs for his tender touch. "Then why let me rephrase my wishes?"

"Because I still don't think your brain comprehends what your heart already knows."

I contemplate his words as I give him complete control over my body. If my heart already knew what my brain does, I wouldn't be dancing with him, trying to decipher what he was saying.

"Stop speaking in riddles," I whisper, feeling my energy waning with every step.

"You know what you want, yet you're too afraid to chase your dreams. You're stuck in your routine, making you miserable, yet you don't want to change anything."

I've chased my dreams and exceeded them with flying colors. I'm proud of my accomplishments, with or without his help. I'm very proud to be the CEO of my indie author bookstore chain.

Nevertheless, what he said is true.

Whatever I'm chasing now, no money can buy— companionship.

"You suck at being supportive," I growl, and this time when he spins me, I can feel the liquid in my stomach rotate with me.

Perhaps this wedding is my wake-up call—a sign that there is still love and happiness in this world, even amid heartache and uncertainty. With that thought in mind, I allow myself to surrender to the music as I promise myself that once I return home, I'll find someone worth returning home to, no matter how long it will take me.

"He's messing with your head," Evander says when the song ends, pulling me out of my trance.

I don't have to be a genius to know his mind returned to Leon.

Chuckling, I shake my head. "What are you? Some kind of relationship expert?"

Evander doesn't smile this time. "I've seen enough

relationships fail to know that a second chance rarely plays out. If he loved you, he wouldn't have waited a year to tell you." He exhales sharply. "I would cross seas and mountains if I was in his shoes."

"But you're not," I reply, letting his hand go as a sharp pain stings my heart. "And don't worry, I'll never take him back."

NINETEEN

I feel Leon's hateful stare burning into my skin as I sit down with a water bottle in hand. If he came here intending to win me back, he was wrong. I don't owe him anything.

And even though I entertained the thought of seeing where this weekend takes us, it was the eye-opener I needed to close that chapter of my life finally.

"Are you having fun?" my brother asks, rocking Emily on his hip to the beat of the music in the background.

"More or less," I reply, watching Emily's sparkling eyes.

"So, what are you still doing here? The formal part is over. You can leave."

"Is it that obvious?" I ask, flashing my teeth at him while I search for Evander. He was supposed to grab me another water, and since he persisted in doing it the human way, he told me to stay put until he was back.

"That you don't want to be here?" Atlas asks, looking up at

the ceiling. "I think everyone can see that your social meter is below zero." He chuckles, shaking Emily, who giggles with him. "You don't have to stay for the sake of Adde. You've given her enough and some."

The worst part is that she doesn't know how much this weekend has cost me. Not money, but emotions.

"She looks so happy," I say, my gaze falling on her as she dances around River, his hair now loosely flying around.

"She does," Atlas agrees, still bouncing Emily. "And it won't change if you take a well-deserved break."

"Are you trying to get rid of me?" I laugh, rising to my feet. "If so, you're doing a fantastic job."

"Oh no," he replies, grabbing my shoulder. "But I know this is your first weekend off in a long time, and you should enjoy it. You can't water from an empty bucket."

Squeezing his hand, I look deep into his amber eyes, our mother's eyes. "Please tell her I had to go," I say, smiling at him before I grab my faux fur to brace myself for the cold.

"Carena, please let us talk about it," Leon says as he follows me to the door after I couldn't locate Evander. "The thought of losing you made me act irrationally."

"Just stay away from me," I say over my shoulder, picking up pace.

I swear, if he doesn't stop, I'll kick his ass in front of all the guests.

"Please," he says behind me, and I come to an abrupt halt when a large hand cups my chin.

"She'll never be yours again because she's mine," a male voice growls back, and before I can rip myself free, Evander wraps his other arm around me, pulls me in, and presses his lips against mine.

I can't breathe.

The smell of vanilla and smoke envelopes me as he presses me even tighter against his chest while our lips connect. They are soft and feel foreign and yet so familiar.

After the initial shock wears off, I close my eyes and let my intuition guide me. I wrap my arms around his neck, pulling him into me with every fiber of my body.

I shouldn't be entertaining Evander's behavior since he didn't ask for my permission. Still, the longer we stand intertwined, the more I realize I'm not fighting back because I've been dreaming of this moment since he got control of my remote.

What started as a diversion turns into a heated kiss. My mind wanders off when his tongue parts my lips, meeting mine with the taste of wine, fruity and sweet.

"Get off her," Leon yells, grabbing me by the shoulder to rip me away from Evander. His nails dig into my skin, making me yelp.

"How dare you touch her," Evander growls back as he lets go of me, his massive hand closing around Leon's neck. "Let her go."

Leon's grasp on my shoulder loosens slightly. "You wouldn't dare hurt me in front of her entire family," he croaks out, curling his fingers around Evander's arm to ease the pressure.

Leon's grip on me releases, and I rub my shoulder as Evander squeezes his neck.

"Want me to prove you wrong?" Evander spits out, the veins on his hands showing how much strength he's applying.

"That's enough," I cut in, stepping between them, my back to Leon to find Evander's gaze. "I think he got it."

The darkness in Evander's eyes almost scares me—almost because once our eyes lock, the softness I'm used to seeing in him returns.

Leon stumbles forward, bouncing into my back when Evander releases him. After straightening himself, he points at Evander but looks at me. "That's the kind of man you're into? He tried to kill me."

Evander's laugh reverberates through my body. "Don't be dramatic. All I did was bruise your ego," he replies, looking past me at him.

Leon rubs his neck as he points at me. "I'll tell everyone about this. Everyone will know what happened."

An icy shiver runs down my spine.

This is precisely what I was trying to avoid. I didn't want to be the center of attention in another family drama. Not at my sister's wedding.

My eyes scan the happily dancing crowd behind us. If I'm lucky, no one saw our minor disagreement, and since I'm only stuck here for a few more hours, I can make it work. If I leave now, I don't have to face the guests again, and I'll be gone before the rumor of my fake boyfriend can make the rounds.

Just as I'm about to shift my focus back on Leon, I lock eyes with Aunt Margaret; from the looks of it, she's seen it all. Her eyes shift back and forth between my shoulder and Leon, while her mouth stands open as she stirs her martini with her finger.

"Good luck with that," I say to Leon, grabbing Evander's hand to pull him with me.

I can hear Leon gasping for air as he searches for a response to throw at me, and when he swears, I know he saw my aunt.

Aunt Margaret will spread what just happened to everyone who will listen. There's no need to defend myself because she'll ensure everyone hears every little detail of how Leon treated me.

I burst through the door, internally laughing. Leon deserves it. Come morning, his reputation will be null.

"You don't know how long I've been waiting for this moment," Evander says, his breath caressing my face as he closes the door behind us, the cold air biting my injured shoulder. He leans down, his lips hovering only inches away from mine, as if this is his way to seek my silent approval.

This should be the moment I tell him it was a onetime thing. There's no difference in the behavior Leon showed in my direction from what Evander did to him. They both showed aggression. It's a red flag.

And yet…

Evander only threatened him because Leon hurt me— mentally and physically.

But does that justify his reaction? How is it okay for him to act violently, but the same doesn't apply to Leon?

How does—

My eyes wander over his face, closed eyes, and then his lips.

I don't know how my encounter with Leon would have played out if it hadn't been for him. Evander reacted because he was provoked, and his action might not have been ideal, but he did it to protect me. He came to my aid, and it's my turn to repay him.

Instead of talking, I let actions speak as I wrap my arms around his neck again and pull him in.

TWENTY

As the snow falls softly around us, Evander carries me through the pristine white landscape toward my cabin without breaking our kiss. His strong arms cradle me gently, ensuring warmth and comfort in the chilly air as my legs are hitched around his waist. With each step, he carefully navigates the uneven terrain, our breaths forming clouds in the frosty night every time we break apart to gasp for air.

Our kiss becomes rougher, more needy and a bolt of sheer lust travels to my lower belly as I feel his cock press against my pussy through his pants and my dress. Without control, my fingers dig into his dark hair as I grind myself against him, feeling the rugged outline of his tip brushing against my already swollen clit.

I want him.

I need him…inside me.

NOW!

When I open my mouth to tell him, his tongue silences me.

Upon reaching the cabin, he gently lowers me onto the couch beside the fireplace. With a wave of his hand, he conjures flames to life, the fire casting a warm glow across the room. I watch in awe as he works his magic, my eyes drawn to the mesmerizing dance of the flames.

"Have you done this before?" I ask, studying the man far too handsome to be human.

He raises an eyebrow. "Fuck?" he asks, and the word makes my vagina drip with need. He has been so polite, too polite for my taste. So when he says *fuck*—not making love or sex—like it's the most normal thing in his vocabulary, I know I'm about to meet a side of him I haven't seen yet.

"Yes," I moan, watching as a stain of pre-cum stains his pants.

"Not as a djinn," he says, drawling the words because he knows what it will do to me. Knowing that I'll be his first sends another wave of desire through my body.

"So, you're a virgin?" I tease, slowly leaning back.

"As many times as I've watched you get fucked by someone else, I have to say no," he grins, grabbing his dick through his pants.

My cheeks blush at his words.

Is he serious? Does he have the ability to be with me even though I didn't summon him? Has he been shadowing me without me knowing?

If that's true, that means he has watched me getting laid. He could have been there when I got pleasured by other males and even at my own hand.

"Don't be embarrassed," he says, slowly moving his hand up and down his shaft. "I've had enough time to study you."

This should alarm me...instead, it turns me on, knowing he could have been in a dark corner massaging his dick.

"Did you like what you saw?" I ask, taken aback by how bold my question is.

"I would say it prepared me to fuck you like no one has done before," he growls, and the need to touch him slams so hard into me that my body jolts at the thought.

As the fire baths the room in its comforting light, Evander begins to undress, shedding his jacket and then his shirt. My gaze lingers on him, my heart quickening at the sight of his dark hair and piercing dark eyes before they move to his muscular chest and abdomen.

There's an air of mystery about him, a sense of power and allure that captivates me. He's fucking stunning.

If someone had told me how ripped genies are, I would have gone looking for him way sooner.

"Touch yourself," he growls. His gaze follows my hands as I massage my breasts, applying just the right amount of pressure.

"Is this what you want?" he asks, his fingers resting on his belt buckle.

"Yes," I say between ragged breaths as my pussy gradually dampens my panties.

"I didn't catch that," he teases, tapping a finger against the buckle. "Say it. Say what you want. Wish for it, Darling."

I can feel the wetness between my legs as he says those words. He's not even in reach, and my pussy can't decide if she wants his tongue or his dick first.

"I wish you had no clothes on," I pant, my eyes resting on this belt where his dick waits to be released.

In a millisecond, his pants, shoes, and socks disappear, leaving him butt-ass naked. My chest grows heavy as my eyes land on his cock, and pure need rushes through my veins when I see him stroking himself.

Oh my gosh! He's gorgeous! Long, thick, and the tip glistens with the same desire rushing out of me.

Another stroke.

Shit! He can't start without me. This is my favorite part.

I scramble to my knees, my already wet panties sticking to my folds. "A little help, please," I groan, trying to reach the zipper on my backside, but as much as I try, I can't reach it.

"Wish, Darling, wish."

God damnit.

Is he going to do this all night? I still owe him a favor, and if I keep using wishes for small things, I'll be bound to him for eternity.

"I wish I was naked," I say, clenching my teeth.

I didn't have another chance. By the time I'm out of this dress without help, he's probably already done if he keeps stroking himself like that.

My knees press into the couch as my dress vanishes, and for a split second, I have the urge to cover my body from his prying eyes. Yet, when I see his thirsty stare studying my body, a sense of lust rolls through me.

He already has seen it all. He probably has seen every angle of me while I was busy chasing an orgasm.

I lean back and slowly open my legs.

"Come here," I whisper as I run a trail with my fingers down my belly to my core.

"Do it," he replies, his gaze following my hand's movement.

No, I'm not pleasuring myself again. I started that last night and still remember how it all played out. I can't come again. Not without him inside me.

That's when it hits me.

"I wish you were between my legs, your cock pressing against my pussy," I say, watching him intently.

My muscles tense as I prepare myself for his sudden movement to grant my wish, and I'm confused when I see him strolling in my direction instead.

So he can manipulate the speed of my wish.

Good to know.

He kneels between my legs, his erection pointing at my face as his hungry gaze darts over me. "What's your wish?" he asks when our eyes finally meet.

I can see his lust, his desire to touch every part of my body. Yet, he refrains himself.

"I wish you do whatever you like," I say, spreading my legs even wider, and the pressure in my lower belly builds up when his eyes land on my pussy.

I'm sure he can see the wetness dripping out of me.

"Whatever I like?" he teases, pressing his lips together in the last attempt to keep his self-control in check.

"Don't make me regret that wish," I add, pressing my ass lower so my backside connects with his thighs.

When our skin meets, I see the light in his eyes shift. It's like every ounce of manners he had disappeared and is replaced by sheer desire.

I gasp as my ass is being lifted into the air without him moving a muscle. My back arches as my pussy comes closer and closer to his cock, and I feel tightness and pressure building in my core when his dick is only inches away from my entrance.

Without warning, a pile of pillows appears beneath my ass, and I let out another gasp when he releases his magic on me, and I sink into his makeshift wedge beneath me.

"I want to see when you come undone," he moans, his hands

finding a hold on my hips.

Instinctively, I want to move even closer to him to bridge the gap between us, but he's faster. Evander grips his dick and drags the head over my clit, breaking the small part of composure I still have left.

I'm needy and already halfway to my orgasm, and he hasn't even started yet. This is going way faster than it has the right to be.

"I need you inside me," I moan, closing my eyes to focus on his touch.

As he drags his cock through my folds, coating the tip with my slickness, a fire ignites in my veins.

"Like this?" he breathes deeply as he slides into me agonizingly slow.

I moan as he pushes into me, deep and slow. I feel how his dick stretches me, gliding past the spot that is already tingling, ready to release the tension that has been building up since our first kiss.

Another wave of pleasure escapes my throat when I feel the pressure of his entire cock inside me, and he drags it backward slowly.

"Stop teasing me," I groan as panic grips me when I feel the emptiness he's leaving behind as he almost pulls out. I want to grab his hips and thrust him into me relentlessly until I finally fall over the edge.

Evander has other plans.

"How long until you start screaming my name?" he asks, and I can hear the smile through his words as he steadily presses into me again.

"Long. Very long," I lie, biting my lip.

"Don't lie," he replies, pulling back, and when his hips move down on me again, he releases my right hip and repositions his hand on my lower belly. I inhale sharply when I feel his thumb applying pressure to my clit, sending sparks straight to the full feeling inside me. In response, my pussy clenches around him, almost forcing him to stay in place.

"Oh, you like that?" he moans, and it's the first sign, besides his hard cock, that he's enjoying this as much as I do. "Relax, Darling. This orgasm is just the beginning," he adds, pumping into me.

Every fiber of my body goes wild as he rubs his thumb over my clit in a circular motion while picking up the pace. My pussy clenches around him with every stroke of his thumb, and I have to open my eyes because the feeling of him thrusting into me is too much.

His raven black hair bounces with his rhythm, and my core reaches a boiling state when I see his teeth biting down on his lip in concentration as he takes me, deep thrust after deep thrust.

"Harder," I whisper, even though the slapping noise of my ass clapping against his legs is deafening.

I want every inch of him, every ridged, rock-hard inch!

"Darling. Say it," he grunts, grabbing my hip harder, and I'm sure he'll leave a permanent mark on me.

"I wish you would fuck me harder," I groan, arching against him with each word that comes over my lips.

Only a few more thrusts and I feel the tension, the delicious torture of my needy desire pulsating inside me. Evander rolls his hips against me, thrusting upwards, and I'm done for.

I cry out when the vibration of my orgasm starts in my thighs, working its way up to my pussy and core until I spasm. With every roll of his hips, I buck against him, chasing my high, and in an instant, my clit is on fire, too sensitive to be touched and yet wanting to be rubbed stronger.

Evander seems to be aware of my dilemma and stops rubbing while slowing down his thrusting when I collapse beneath him.

"Don't stop," I say breathlessly, watching his dark eyes devour me.

"Darling, now it's my turn," he replies, grabbing my leg, and I whimper when he pulls out and flips me around, my face pressing into the couch.

I gasp when he grasps my hips and pulls my ass against him, his cock finding my still throbbing entrance with one thrust.

Holy fuck!

He warned me. He told me he knew exactly what I liked and was correct. Two orgasms later—one with a remote and one entirely lured out by his dick—he still hasn't gotten his, and I feel shitty about it. I know nothing about him. Does he have a kink? Is there something in particular he likes?

Those thoughts subside when he reaches forward to cup my breast while his other hand pulls and slams me into him relentlessly.

I might not know what he likes, but he does.

Somehow, I expected him to be sensitive about my well-being, giving me a few seconds to recoup…

I'm wrong.

"Don't hold back," Evander grunts behind me, pounding into me, filling my pussy with his cock over and over again to chase his release. "I want to feel your pussy clenching around my cock as I come, sucking up every drop of my cum until you're full."

Again: Holy fuck!

There's nothing gentle about Evander left as he slams into me, and I groan when he releases my breast and fists my hair, pulling my head back.

"I said, don't hold back," he whispers into my ear through ragged breaths. "I want to hear you. I want everyone to know what you're doing to me."

What I am doing to *him*?

It hurts when he lifts my head even a little higher, but it's a pain that sends my pussy clenching for more, and he grunts when a moan escapes my throat with his next push into me.

I love how he's taking from me what he wants. I expected to guide him through every step; him slowing down for me to reassure him he does exactly what I want him to do, asking me if it feels good, and listening to my every wish.

Apparently, that doesn't apply to sex because this is hotter and rougher than anything I've experienced before. He's as desperate to get his as I am, losing all sense of modesty.

With every thrust, a moan escapes my throat. The noise is foreign to me because never—and I mean never—have I let myself lose control.

Warmth builds up in my lower belly again once I get used to letting my desperate cries ring in my ears.

The louder I moan, the harder he thrusts.

I contemplate for a heartbeat to grab his hand and guide it down to my clit, but he has done his job. Now it's time for him to come, and if I get mine before him, that's great.

Pressing my face into the soft couch, I wiggle my hand through between the pillows and my body until my fingers reach my throbbing clit.

"Rub that pussy for me," Evander groans, finally releasing my hair to grab my hip again. "Come for me again!"

He knows exactly what I'm doing.

When I stroke over my already hyper-sensitive clit, a bolt of electricity jolts through me. At this point, I don't care how stupid I sound or look; all I want is for him to release inside me. I want to feel his warm liquid filling me until it drips out of me.

I close my eyes again to redirect all my senses to the friction between us. His thrusts get harder, more desperate, and I'm turned on when I hear him grunting behind me, taking what he needs.

"You're so fucking tight," he groans. "You don't know how long I've been waiting for this. My cock inside you. You riding up against me."

If he says one more word, I'll explode again.

"Oh, Carena. You're perfect," he moans, and another orgasm wrecks my body…and, with it, his.

Evander's cock seems to double in size as he takes deep, forceful thrusts, his grunts reverberating off the walls. I feel his cum spraying into me, each roll of his hip squeezing another wave of his pleasure out of him.

Panting, my body goes slack under him as he pulls out of me, his hands pressing into my ass.

"Are you okay?" he whispers, breathless, as he slumps onto the couch beside me.

I can't move. I can't talk. Every working body part is exhausted and yet screaming for more.

"Not okay, but satisfied," I groan, trying to flip onto my back, but my muscles won't listen.

"Oh, Darling. I'm not done with you yet," he whispers into my ear, sending a shiver down my spine.

TWENTY-ONE

Draped in a blanket, I curl Evander's soft hair around my finger as he watches me tentatively.

"Want to recreate our first night here?" I ask, feeling the warmth of the fire crackling behind me.

"Go on," he muses, his fingers trailing over my nipple through the blanket.

"Never have I ever had sex in a hot tub," I say, my eyes lingering on him.

"I like where this is going," he replies, smirking at me.

This is risky. I'm playing with fire, and I'm not afraid to get burned.

Knowing that someone could catch us adds a thrill I didn't even know I had in me. But no one should see us since the tub is located at the backside of my cabin towards a distant forest.

"Whoever gets there first can pick the position," I shout, jumping to my feet. On my way to the door, I hold on to the old scratchy blanket and swear under my breath as I try to wrap it tighter around me. When I rip the door open, I look over my shoulder and see Evander still lying on the couch. Chuckling, I slam the door shut behind me and slip around the corner on a patch of ice. A gasp escapes my throat as I try to keep my balance, and when I look up at the hot tub, I let out a single chuckle.

"Well played," I say, tiptoeing as fast as I can to the steaming waters, the snow crunching softly beneath my feet.

"What should I pick?" Evander asks as he leans against the tub shell, his arms resting on the plastic outstretched. "How about you on your knees?"

The snow beneath my feet has nothing on the radiating heat surging through my pussy. As much as I want to obey his wish, two can play this game.

I literally jump into the hot tub to get my feet off the cold ground and immediately regret my decision when a prickling feeling rushes through them. Biting on my lip, I breathe through the uncomfortable feeling as the warmth seeps into my bones.

"Actually," I begin, tilting my chin up. "I wish to ride you."

He thinks he has won our little challenge by using his magic, but my wishes trump his power any day. Plus, he already had me on my knees.

"Fuck," he growls, his nostrils flaring as his eyes wander over me.

I watch him as he tries to disobey my wish. Every muscle in

his body tenses as he fights to stay in control.

"Don't fight it, Darling," I grin, moving over to him. "Once I get mine, you can do whatever you want with me," I add, placing my knees around his thighs.

I lower myself, and my core heats when I feel his cock at my entrance. Slowly, I let myself down on him, his dick stretching my pussy wide.

"You like this?" I ask, slowly picking up pace. The water threatens to wash over the shell as I move, taking him inch by inch.

"I'll never get enough of you," he growls as he bites into my collarbone. I moan when his teeth connect with my skin, but it isn't pain rushing through me but arousal.

After a few seconds, his large hands grip my hips as he picks me up and lets me down on his cock to his desire. Arching back, I position myself so his dick brushes against my most sensitive spot, sending waves of pleasure through me each time his tip touches it.

Fucking a djinn, a mythical creature that shouldn't exist in the human world, shouldn't feel this good.

But it does.

With each stroke, I can feel another orgasm creeping closer. The thought of getting caught adds to the pleasure I'm feeling.

I always play it safe, never leaving room for errors, so why am I acting so out of character? What is it about him that makes me forget about all the virtues I have?

"Do you enjoy riding me?" he asks, cupping my breast, and I jolt back when he leans down, taking my nipple in with his lips.

Oh god. This isn't good.

Giving him access to my nipples won't play out in my favor. Plus, his cock doesn't go deep enough in this position. I want his hilt to slam into me, pounding my ass like there's no tomorrow.

"I do, but this isn't enough," I moan as he gently bites my nipple while massaging the other.

Somehow, gracefully, I lift my leg over his lap and spin around, positioning my ass against his abdomen.

"Now that's new," he laughs, grabbing my hips.

"I need you deeper," I whisper, grabbing his dick through my legs, and with practiced ease, I slide onto him.

I rotate and roll my hips, pressing his cock into my walls to find my G-spot. When his tip brushes against it, I let out a moan and am surprised to find his hand stifling the sound.

"We can't have them catch us," Evander groans into my ear as he leans forward, curling his arm around my belly and pinning me against him. "Just be a good little Darling and ride me until you come."

Fuck!

Does he know what his words do to me? Is that why he's saying them, or does it come naturally to him?

Moving in water is so much more challenging than expected.

My legs shake as I lower myself onto him, over and over again, taking him in. But I don't care. Even if I can't walk tomorrow because I'm beyond sore, it's worth it.

"Let me help you," he whispers into my ear, slowly releasing my mouth. "But you have to promise me to be silent. You can scream all you want when we're back inside."

My body tenses when his fingers brush against my clit, caressing it in a circular motion.

He knows my weakness. He knows that by rubbing my clit, he'll cut my time in half, maybe even more.

I use the momentum of the splashing water to bounce on him, leaning forward as much as his arms allow me. While his right hand is busy, he uses his left to move me against him until we come to a rhythm.

I get bold when I feel the all-consuming pressure and heat building in my core. I reach between my legs and hear Evander's raspy moan when I curl my hand around his testicles. As I massage them, I feel his pleasure throbbing through them, and I'm fascinated by how soft yet firm his balls feel in my hand.

"You're going to be the death of me," he growls, biting into my shoulder blade, and the pain shoots me right over the edge.

I can't move as my orgasm rolls through me, but that doesn't stop Evander from chasing his. He bounces me on his lap until his breath comes out hot and desperate as he releases inside me.

As we relax in the soothing heat, I gaze up at the night sky, the stars twinkling brightly overhead. It's a moment of tranquility, peace, and contentment away from the hustle and bustle of the world. In the distance, the faint sound of music drifts through the air, the afterparty of the wedding still ringing in my ears.

Lost in the beauty of the moment, Evander turns his head to me, his eyes full of curiosity and longing. "What do you see in your future?" he asks softly, his voice carrying across the water.

He says something else, but I can't hear his words through the splashing water.

I pause, considering his question carefully. I've never been one to dwell too much on the future, preferring to live in the present moment. But there is something about the way he asked, the earnestness in his gaze, that makes me want to open up to him.

"I want adventure," I say, looking up at the stars. "I want to explore unknown places and experience new things. I want to live life to the fullest, with no regrets."

Evander nods, his expression thoughtful. "I understand," he replies, his voice tinged with a hint of sadness. "But sometimes, the greatest adventures are the ones we have right before us."

My stomach drops as his words float through my mind,

repeating them repeatedly. No matter how I rearrange them, they have the same meaning, one that I don't want to hear.

"This," I wiggle my finger between us, "it's never going to happen again," I continue, panic rising inside me.

"Where are you going?" Evander asks as I climb out of the tub to grab the blanket I discarded hastily on the ground when I jumped in.

"I need to get some sleep. Tomorrow will be a long day," I reply, digging my feet into the ground to get as much distance between us as possible.

As I slip into the cabin, I hear the laughter and music from the main cabin. Just a few hours ago, I was in there, miserable and waiting for my time to check out. Between now and then, something has shifted inside me. I'm still the same person I was when I arrived here two days ago, but something changed, and I can't figure out what it is.

I shake my head to scatter that thought.

Once morning comes, I'll throw my bag into the car and peel out of the driveway to return home, leaving everything that happened this weekend behind.

TWENTY-TWO

The horn blares as I bang my fists against the smooth leather.

"You said you would take care of the snow," I groan through clenched teeth, glaring at Evander.

"I did, but you never said when it should stop."

"I can't be stuck here. I have meetings to attend and deadlines to uphold."

In the dim light of the early morning, I hurriedly tossed my luggage into the back of the Jeep, my breath visible in the chilly air. I was eager to leave, to escape the confines of the mountains and the memories it now holds. But as I settled into the driver's seat and turned the key, my heart sank.

The engine sputtered to life, but when I tried to pull away, the wheels spun uselessly in the snow.

The road, buried beneath a thick blanket of white and ice, is nowhere to be seen. Frustration bubbles up inside me, mingling with a sense of helplessness. I've been so focused on Leon and Evander that I didn't consider the possibility of being snowed in.

Turning to Evander, I let out a guttural exhale. "I wish for the road to be cleared."

He shakes his head, his expression apologetic. "I'm sorry, but I can't do that," he says softly. "The snowfall was too heavy, and I can't make it disappear without someone noticing."

My frustration grows, my mind racing with thoughts of everything I left behind. I have been determined to put distance between myself and my past to start fresh once I return home.

But now, I'm trapped on the mountain with my family, ex, and a man I still barely know.

As the reality of my situation sinks in, I feel a wave of despair wash over me. How can I possibly endure another day or two in this place, surrounded by memories I want to forget?

But then, as I look around at the snow-covered landscape, something shifts inside me. Despite my initial reluctance, I find myself drawn to the quiet beauty of the mountain, to the sense of peace that seems to settle over everything. And as I glance at Evander beside me, I realize that perhaps being stuck here isn't such a bad thing after all. Maybe, just maybe, it's exactly where I'm meant to be.

With a sigh, I turn the car off, my expression softening. "I guess we'll just have to make the best of it," I say, a hint of a smile playing at the corners of my lips.

He returns my smile, his eyes sparkling with warmth. "I think we can manage that," he replies, reaching out to squeeze my hand, but I pull away before he can touch me.

"Ok, new plan," I reply after a deep breath. "I might be unable to leave, but that doesn't mean I can't do my work from here. All I need is a stable signal."

"I don't know where you're going with this, but go on."

"Your job is to keep my family away from my cabin while I work."

"I don't think—"

"You can have the main room while I work from the library. Once the sun clears the road, we can get out of here. So, I wish for a cloudless day," I say, closing my eyes.

"I really think this isn't what the universe is trying to tell you."

"The universe has nothing to do with this," I reply, glaring at him. "I have to work with what I'm giving, and right now, I need to focus on my work."

He bites his lip. "Alright. I'll keep your family off your back," he says, opening his door. "You know, you can't run forever," he adds before slamming it shut.

What the hell is his problem?

I'm not running from anything.

Does he know how hard it is to lead a successful business? Luckily, I love what I do—owning a bookstore chain has always been a big dream of mine. But this dream comes with a lot of responsibilities.

I roll my eyes when I see Evander stroll past my cabin toward the big one. I gave him explicit instructions: stay in my cabin and keep them away from me while keeping him close. Now, in just a few seconds, my family will hear the news from him: all of us are stuck on this mountain until the roads are clear.

I want to run after him and stop him, but they will find out sooner rather than later once they try to leave. Plus, I'm still processing what happened last night. If I catch up to him, I don't know if I'll be able to keep my emotions in check since I'm trying so hard to tell myself that I don't need him.

He's not human. I need to remember that before my heart gets me in trouble.

Sure, I'm attracted to him, but who wouldn't? If he pressed me against a wall or door frame, I'd spread my legs for him like a good little Darling because I want him to take me; I want to see what he will do to me. I loved his darker side too much, the way he fisted my hair, how he flung me around like he couldn't live another minute without being inside me.

My vagina clenches.

Traitorous Witch.

She's the one who put me in this predicament. Well, partially, but that's not the point.

The point is, I'm in deep trouble.

This needs to end.

I have to keep him away from the other guests and far away from Leon and everything will be fine. I'll be fine because nothing is going to happen between us again.

As I step out of the car, the morning sun casts a soft golden hue over the tranquil mountains. The crunch of snow under my boots echoes in the morning's quiet stillness. I take a moment to savor the crisp air, relishing the peacefulness of my secluded cabin.

With a sigh, I make my way up the wooden steps, opening the door with a familiar click. Stepping into the cozy interior, I'm greeted by the comforting scent of old books and polished wood.

This is how my arrival was supposed to feel instead of bouncing face-first into my ex with a stranger on my heels.

This weekend was…yeah, I don't have words to describe it…and even though I don't have the physical distance I wanted from it, I have to return to my routine.

I need to get back into work mode.

My first order of business is to check for reception. I'm so used to feeling my phone vibrate for my attention at all hours that it didn't go unnoticed that it hadn't been ringing.

I go into the library and to the large window that overlooks the sprawling forest in the distance, hoping for a single bar. As I glance down at my phone, a flurry of missed messages and calls flood the screen, evidence of the world I momentarily left behind.

Over two hundred messages and thirty-six missed calls. Are they serious?

Just as I'm about to despair, my phone springs to life with the insistent vibration of an incoming call. It's Jinelle, my assistant. I hastily answer, bracing myself for the inevitable onslaught of tasks and deadlines.

"Carena, thank goodness you're finally reachable!" Jinelle's voice crackles through the line, laced with urgency. "We've got a situation here. We need those documents signed for the author we're trying to snag, and there's a whole slew of events happening at the bookstore this week that you've been MIA for."

My brow furrows in concern as I listen to Jinelle's rapid-fire explanation. I quickly grab a nearby sticky note and begin jotting down notes, my mind already racing ahead to prioritize my tasks for the day.

"Alright, Jinelle, I've got it. Send me the documents, and I'll get them signed as soon as possible," I reply, my tone firm. "And let me know what's happening at the bookstore. I'll catch up on everything I've missed."

With a plan in place, I set to work, diving headfirst into the mountain of tasks. Hours pass in a blur as I meticulously review contracts, draft emails, and make phone calls, my focus unwavering despite the distractions that beckon from outside my window.

I could go out there and join the guests in a snowball fight or bring my phone to work from the hot tub, but I can't risk walking into Evander.

As the sun begins its slow descent towards the horizon, casting long shadows across the snowy floor, I finally allow myself a moment's respite. I stretch my cramping muscles and glance around the dimly lit library, realizing with a pang of hunger that I forgot to eat all day.

Setting aside my phone, which I have been glued to throughout the day, I walk towards the entrance door, intent on finding something to satisfy my growling stomach in the big cabin. But as I reach for the handle, something catches my eye.

A warm glow emanates from the small table by the crackling fireplace, illuminating a tempting spread of food that appeared out of nowhere. My breath catches in my throat as I approach, my heart pounding with a mixture of confusion and gratitude.

There, amidst the flickering flames, stands a hearty meal fit for a weary traveler. Steaming bowls of soup, crusty bread, and a decadent slice of pie entice invitingly, filling the cabin with the tantalizing aroma of home-cooked comfort.

For a moment, I stand rooted to the spot, overcome with a sense of wonder at the unexpected gesture of kindness.

If the food is warm, he must still be close. I look around the room to discover I'm the only soul here.

With a soft smile tugging at my lips, I sink into the couch, my mind spiraling back to last night for just a second until I shake it away and savor each delicious bite as I bask in the firelight's warmth.

Evander doesn't even know what this means to me. Not only is this a way of avoiding more drama by staying in my cabin, this also saves me valuable time as I don't have to cabin hop.

As I eat, I can't help but feel a sense of gratitude wash over me. Amid the chaos of the wedding and the demands of my daily life, I have a moment of peace and nourishment, both for my body and soul.

And as the last traces of daylight fade into the night, so does the feeling of being a strong, independent woman. It's the nights that hit me the hardest. I got used to falling asleep alone, but it hurts knowing that I'll wake up by myself.

Stuffing the bread into my mouth, my eyes fall on the book Evander read the first morning. I'm surprised I haven't noticed it earlier since he left it beside the couch on the ground.

I pick it up and flip through the pages, recognizing every word I wrote. I'm not the same woman who wrote this manuscript, yet it's a part of my story. Thinking that writing out my diary through the eyes of an older version of myself would help me process the loss of my mother was my idea of freeing myself of the guilt.

I was wrong.

Without looking, I know exactly how old I made the story's main character.

Thirty.

The exact age my mother was when she went to bed for the last time, and the same age I am now. Knowing that in a few short days, I'll be older than my mother ever turned constricts my airway.

Every parent's wish is for their children to outlive them, but for someone to die so young is cruel and something I'll never understand.

Skimming over the pages, I live through the hardest months of my life in seconds. This book was never supposed to fall into someone else's hands. It was meant for me—me alone.

How much did Evander read?

While sadness slams into me like a tsunami, I also remember how it felt to turn my thoughts and feelings into words and scribble them onto paper. At first, the sentences were covered in tears, but with each page, my heart slowed down, and the pain in my throat lessened.

Why did I stop?

Looking up from the book, I realize I made it back into the library without realizing it. Other people's words and worlds surround me. They made them up to help a person like me forget about reality.

"It wouldn't hurt to start writing again," Evander says from behind me, and I almost jump out of my skin.

"I hate when you do that," I croak out, pressing my book

tightly against my chest as if I can keep the words I wrote inside.

Evander leans against the door, his large body filling in the frame. "What's holding you back?"

I cock my head. "From what?"

"Writing?"

A laugh escapes my throat. "I'm not a writer."

"But you help other authors."

"That's something else. My dream was to help small independent authors to be seen."

"And you are one of them."

"You know what? I'm not in the mood to discuss something I did years ago. This," I hold the book up high, "is nothing close to the phenomenal manuscripts I've read since I opened up my first store."

"What if your book falls into the hands of a reader who shares your pain? What if this book changes a person's life because they realize they're not alone? This manuscript might not be phenomenal for every reader…but for the right one, this will be the best thing they ever read because they can connect to someone."

I let his words sink in.

That's exactly what I was looking for when I wrote all those words. The thought of finding someone who lived through my pain and came out stronger was what I needed twenty years ago, even ten.

But I've made it. I survived.

"Do you charge hourly, or does this session go on the house?" I ask, tucking my book neatly into the empty gap it belongs in on the bottom shelf.

"You could never pay the price for a session with me," Evander responds, his voice teasing.

My cheeks flush. "Why are you here?" I ask, turning to face him after I regain my normal temperature.

"Aunt Margaret made a delicious meal for all of us. She told me to get you."

I wave my hand. "I already ate dinner."

Evander looks over his shoulder at the still-steaming meal on the table. "No, that was lunch." He shakes his head. "It doesn't matter. We have to go now."

"She's going to be fine," I reply, rolling my eyes.

"You don't understand. She threatened that if I don't return with you in tow, she'll sit beside me."

Now, that's a threat I can't ignore.

So far, Evander has done a fantastic job of keeping his lips sealed about our arrangement, so I can't risk him spilling the beans now. Nevertheless, Leon will be there, and I don't know how long I can keep my low-boiling anger for him down.

Evander grins at me. "We just have to show our faces for a minute. I'll say I'm not feeling well, and then we leave."

"Promise?" I ask, holding out my pinky.

"Promise," he responds, staring at my finger, and my cheeks heat again when I realize he has no clue what my gesture means.

TWENTY-THREE

The grand cabin that was adorned with vibrant flowers and twinkling lights less than twenty-four hours ago now stands empty like the beautiful minimalistic skeleton I use for my retreats.

My heart sinks as I notice the familiar faces scattered throughout the room, remnants of the wedding party that lingers behind. But the sight of him sends a shiver down my spine—Leon, his eyes bearing into me with an intensity that makes my skin prickle with discomfort.

With a heavy sigh, I force myself to take a seat at the long wooden table, acutely aware of the weight of everyone's gaze upon me. It's my cabin, my refuge in the mountains, and now, with the snowstorm that raged outside the day before, we're all stranded together, trapped in this confined space with no escape.

Luckily, no one knows that I'm responsible for it.

As I settle into my chair, my aunt's voice pierces through the tense silence, her tone cheerful yet probing. "So, Carena dear, when can we expect to hear wedding bells for you? And what about little ones running around? You're not getting any younger, you know."

For goodness' sake.

Evander's butt cheeks haven't even made contact with his chair, and my aunt comes in guns blazing.

My cheeks flush with embarrassment as I shift uncomfortably in my seat, my mind racing to find a polite yet evasive response. My gaze falls onto my brother, his arms wrapped around little Emily, who is wearing her meal on her face, then to my sister, leaning into her new husband.

Marriage and children are topics I've been avoiding since…well, since Leon. My focus was instead on my career and my independence. The pressure from my family to conform to societal expectations weighs heavily on me, a constant reminder of my perceived shortcomings.

Before I can formulate a reply, a reassuring squeeze on my hand beneath the table catches me off guard. I glance to my side, meeting Evander's. His eyes convey understanding and solidarity, reassuring me I'm not alone in this uncomfortable situation.

Drawing strength from his supportive presence, I manage a small smile as I turn back to her. "Oh, you know me, Aunt Margaret," I reply lightly, my tone carefully measured. "I'm just enjoying the freedom and independence that comes with being a business owner. Who knows what the future holds?"

My aunt's brow furrows in confusion, but before she can press further, the conversation is diverted by Emily tipping over her juice, spilling it all over the table. I breathe a silent sigh of relief, grateful for the temporary reprieve from the interrogation.

As the meal progresses, I'm increasingly grateful for Evander's steadfast presence by my side. His subtle gestures of support—a reassuring squeeze of my hand, a knowing glance— serve as a lifeline in the sea of scrutiny and expectation.

But despite his comforting presence, I can't shake the unease that lingers in the air. The tension between Leon and I crackles, his gaze burning into me with an intensity that makes my skin crawl.

With each passing minute, I feel the weight of my insecurities and uncertainties pressing down on me. Will I ever find the courage to pursue my own happiness, free from the constraints of societal expectations and familial pressure?

"I think this is our cue," I whisper as Atlas cleans off the last drop of juice.

"Just a few more minutes," Evander says, a smile covering his face. "We're just getting to the good part."

My neck whips in his direction when I feel his hand withdraw from mine, and before I can say anything, my stomach tightens as the warmth of his fingers seeps through the thin fabric of my pants.

"What are you doing?" I snarl, pressing my hand on top of his.

"Make me stop," he says, his dark eyes lingering on mine as his fingers trail over my thigh.

My gaze flies over the familiar faces surrounding me. The atmosphere around the dinner table is convivial, filled with the lively chatter of friends and family continuing their normal conversations after pausing for a moment to hear my aunt tear me apart.

"You can't be serious," I whisper as his fingers find the seam of my pants. His warm fingers brush against my belly as he squeezes past the elastic band.

I shift uneasily, my fingers trembling as I try to move away from his touch discreetly. But Evander, sensing my discomfort, seems determined to make his presence known, his digits trailing down my stomach to my vagina with an insistent rhythm.

As the conversations around the table ebb and flow, I grow increasingly anxious, my attention divided between the lively banter above and the mischievous hand below. I reach down to shove him away, hoping to soothe his mischievous idea, but my efforts are in vain as I feel his fingers touch my clit.

With a sudden jolt, two fingers push into me, sending a sharp pang of pleasure shooting up my legs. Reflexively, my knees jerk upwards, colliding with the underside of the table with a resounding thud.

The sudden noise draws the entire table's attention, their eyes turning towards me with curiosity and concern. But it's Leon's gaze that makes my heart skip a beat; his eyes narrowed with suspicion as he studies me, sending a flush creeping up my cheeks.

This can't be happening.

I press my ass into the backrest of the chair, hoping it's enough to let Evander know he needs to stop. Instead, he smiles at me, pumping his fingers into me deeper.

Feeling exposed and vulnerable, I know I have to act fast. With a forced smile, I push the chair back, and once his hand is freed, I rise from my seat, my movements swift and decisive. "I, uh, just remembered that I need to check on something in the kitchen," I stammer, my voice betraying my nerves.

Before anyone can protest, I hastily make my escape, my heart pounding in my chest as I navigate the maze of chairs and bodies. With each step, I feel the weight of Leon's scrutiny bearing down on me.

As I reach the relative safety of the kitchen, I allow myself a moment to catch my breath, my hands trembling with adrenaline as I breathe in and out to calm my nerves.

The door opens behind me, and the instinct to beat the living hell out of Evander shoots through me when I see his smirking face.

"What were you thinking?" I ask, keeping my voice hushed as I point to the table.

"You didn't wish for it to stop," he says, closing the door behind him.

"That's my family out there," I reply, massaging my temple.

"No one noticed," Evander says, closing the distance between us. "I made sure of it," he adds, snapping his fingers.

The thought of someone catching me with his fingers inside me at the dinner table is terrifying…

And so fucking hot.

For a moment, I forgot who he was, and I'm ashamed to say that if I had known that he could have made me come with no one noticing, it was something I didn't think I liked.

No, it's so wrong. I should be disgusted.

"You were so wet," he says, looking at his fingers. "I can still feel your pussy clenching around me."

Nope. I won't do it. I'll walk out of here, lock myself into my cabin, and barricade myself in my room until the roads are clear.

"Your family won't find out, I swear," he says, holding his hands in the air, and I can see the shiny slickness of my pleasure still coating his fingers.

He's giving me enough space and a clear route to burst through that door and into the open. He's letting me go.

I step forward, my eyes glued to the door, grabbing him by his shirt to pull him in.

"If my family finds out, my aunt is the least of your problems," I snarl before lifting my gaze to him.

He glances down at me with wide, innocent eyes, seemingly unaware of the chaos he's causing inside me. With a smile, he scoops me into his arms, cradling me close as he makes his way toward a small, unused wooden table in the far corner of the kitchen.

As he carries me, I can feel his erection press against my pelvis, and the instinct to rub myself against him again almost makes me lose my mind.

My ass collides with the surface, and a shiver runs down my spine when I realize my pants and underwear are gone.

"We don't have much time," he whispers into my ear, hooking his hands under my legs to scoot my ass closer to the edge.

I let out a quiet squeal when I feel the wooden edge bite into my butt, but I don't have enough time to straighten myself because, in the next moment, I feel his cock sliding up and down against my vagina as he searches for my entrance. With each stroke, his tip becomes more sleek until his cock slides into me effortlessly.

I throw my head back as he fills me with his length, his hands grabbing my ass tightly to stop me from moving away from him.

"Tell me you don't like me fucking you," he groans, thrusting into me as he cups my breast.

"I don't," I moan, my nails biting into the wooden surface

beneath me. "Because I fucking love it."

I should wipe that mischievous grin off his face and leave, but his dick feels so good.

He presses me down until my back arches against the table, and desperately, I wrap my legs around his waist, trying to find any purchase as he slams into me.

"I'll never get enough of you," he growls, his hips rolling into me again and again, shaking the entire table.

I feel the pressure building up in my lower belly, slowly radiating into my legs.

"I'm so close," I say between ragged breaths.

When he doesn't answer, I open my eyes. My moan catches in my throat when I notice someone standing before the closed door.

I don't know how long Leon has been standing in the kitchen, watching Evander thrust into me relentlessly.

My mouth opens to give Evander a signal that we have to stop immediately, but with the next pump of his hips, I feel the orgasm ripple through my lower belly. Evander presses his hands against my lips to muffle the loud moan rippling through me, and my eyes tear as I try to hold Leon's gaze.

"Come for me, Darling," Evander whispers into my ear, moving his cock in a circular motion, and each time his dick brushes against my G-spot, I arch against him, my body demanding more.

A tear rolls out of the corner of my eye when the waves of pleasure finally subside, and without giving him any instructions, Evander pulls out of me, leaving my pussy throbbing.

"We're done," Leon yells, ripping the door open and slamming it shut behind him.

I punch my fist into Evander's chest and bite into his finger when I see the satisfied smile on his face. "You said no one would catch us," I hiss after he removed his hand from my face.

"I said *your family won't find out*. Ex-fiancés don't make the cut as family members," he replies, pushing a strand of hair behind my ear. "And that wasn't my doing. He was here because you let him in."

"This isn't funny," I snarl, searching the ground for my pants until I realize I didn't take them off. "Give me my pants back. I need to go out there and de-escalate the situation before he tells everyone what we just did."

"He won't tell anyone," Evander says, carefully stepping away, and I'm surprised to find myself dressed again.

"Why are you so fucking calm?"

"Because I ensured he can't tell anyone what he saw," he replies, and with a blink of his eye, we're fully dressed again.

I shake my head. "Did you know he was standing there?"

Evander doesn't answer.

My voice reaches a new high pitched squeaking sound. "For how long?"

"Does it matter?"

It doesn't, but it feels wrong and...I don't know the right word. Scandalous? Shocking? Thrilling?

What the fuck is wrong with me?

Did I really just get off from knowing that my ex has been watching us? Seeing the horror in his eyes activated something inside me I didn't think I had. It's like a switch clicked inside my head, finally bringing a chapter of my life to an end I thought I had ended months ago.

A wide range of emotions rush through my body when I try to pinpoint what to feel.

"This is wrong," I say, shaking my head at Evander. "This should have never happened."

I don't give him a chance to answer because I'm out the door the next moment, bolting past the gawking people at the dinner table.

TWENTY-FOUR

*G*reat.

I did it again.

While the wedding guests might not know what conspired inside the kitchen, they for sure noticed me bulldozing out of the cabin into the open.

The rumor mill is probably running hot as I slam the door to my cabin shut and barricade myself in my room.

I lock both entrances this time, but it doesn't make me feel any better. If Evander wants to get in here, he will because doors didn't seem to hold him back when he used to stalk before I even knew he existed.

I'm so angry, I want to scream and pull my hair. Instead, I rummage through the nightstand to find the tiniest journal hidden inside the drawer.

If I want to stay level-headed while being stuck here, I need to clear my mind, and the only thing I can think of is to scribble down my feelings.

But what do I feel?

My focus shifts to a metallic reflection gleaming in the corner of my eye every time I shift. As I follow the distracting light, my gaze falls on the golden-green lamp half submerged in my suitcase, hidden partially beneath my clothes.

The urge to touch it tingles my fingers, but I restrain myself from caving.

Why am I doing this to myself? Why can't I just be happy?

The soft glow of lamplight casts a warm embrace over the dimly lit bedroom as I nestle beneath the covers, a tangle of sheets and emotions. With a heavy sigh, I reach for the pen attached to the worn journal, its pages a repository for the whirlwind of feelings I've been bottling up for far too long.

As my pen hovers over the blank page, my mind is awash with a tumult of thoughts and emotions, each one vying for attention amidst the cacophony of my racing thoughts. For years, I've been searching for meaning and purpose, grappling with the weight of expectations and the fear of disappointment. I thought I had it all figured out.

I created a great life for myself.

I love my job—maybe not the hours and workload—but I knew what I signed up for when I opened my first Indie Inkpot.

And I love…

As much as I try to focus on something non-work-related, I

come up short. Besides my stores, there's nothing that brings me joy.

With a determined exhale, I write, my pen tracing the contours of my innermost thoughts with a raw honesty that borders on desperation. Every word is a revelation, a confession of the dissatisfaction and longing that has been simmering beneath the surface.

"I don't know what I want," I scrawl across the page, my handwriting shaky with uncertainty. "I feel like I'm stuck in this endless cycle of monotony, trapped in a life that no longer feels like my own."

As the words spill forth, my heart clenches with longing, a yearning for something more, something beyond the confines of my mundane existence. And with each sentence I pen, I find myself drawn back to one recurring theme—family.

While I could strangle Adde on most days and dodge my father's phone calls, I would do anything for them. The same goes for my brother and the most precious little girl he helped create. And while the backbone of my happiness should be my family, I can't ignore the silent voice inside my head that helped shape me into the woman I am now.

No, it wasn't a voice that supported me through my darkest times; it was a presence I could feel, but never see; a person I thought I made up, but was always real.

Evander.

A whirlwind of energy and unpredictability, a force of nature that swept into my life like a hurricane, leaving chaos and exhilaration in his wake. Something about his untamed spirit ignites a spark within me, a sense of freedom and possibility I've long forgotten.

But even as I pour my heart onto the page, I can't shake the unsettling fear that lingers deep in my consciousness—the fear of admitting my true feelings, of embracing the vulnerability that comes with opening my heart to another.

"He makes me feel alive," I confess, my pen trembling. "I love his uncontrollable nature, his zest for life. But I'm scared— scared of what it means to admit that I want more, scared of risking everything for a chance at happiness."

As the weight of my confession settles over me, I feel a surge of conflicting emotions—fear, longing, hope.

For so long, I've been trapped in a cycle of self-doubt and indecision, afraid to take the leap into the unknown.

But as I lie in the quiet stillness of my room, surrounded by the echo of my thoughts, I know I can't continue to ignore the stirring in my heart. I owe it to myself to embrace the uncertainty to take a chance on happiness, even if it means breaking down the hard barrier I've built around my heart.

I close the journal, my heart pounding in my chest. It feels like I'm thirteen again, writing the name of my crush into my diary in case the sheer thought of him would make my dreams come true.

But I'm not thirteen anymore. I'm a grown woman who knows that happy endings aren't real. Yes, he might be a djinn, a being that doesn't belong to my world, and precisely because of that, this will never work out.

Tomorrow is a new day. If the roads aren't good enough to travel, I'll start hiking or rolling down the mountain because if I'm stuck here for one more day so close to my family, Evander, and Leon, I'll lose my mind.

As I drift off to sleep, a faint smile tugs at the corners of my lips, fueled by the escape plan to get back to what I know best—loneliness.

TWENTY-FIVE

I peer through the window of my childhood home. Outside, under the expansive canopy of a towering oak tree, a figure catches my attention.

A woman stands beneath the tree, her long, flowing dress swaying gently in the breeze. From this distance, she seems like a timeless apparition as I watch her, the seasons shifting around the figure, a subtle dance of time unfolding before my eyes.

Who is she?

I squint my eyes to get a better look at her, and my heart jumps when I see two children frolicking around the serene figure. One, a girl of about ten, darts and weaves through the dappled sunlight of spring, her laughter ringing out like crystal chimes. Beside her, a smaller girl, perhaps six years old, giggles uncontrollably as she chases after her older sister. Nearby, a little boy, no more than three years old, sits on the ground, engrossed in the simple pleasure of playing with rocks.

I feel a tug at my heartstrings as I watch them. Memories flood my mind, transporting me back to a time when I, too, played beneath that same tree, surrounded by the love and warmth of my siblings.

But it's the figure beneath the oak that holds my gaze captive.

As I study her, a pang of recognition shoots through me. The features, though softened by time, are unmistakable. Long, dark hair cascades over slender shoulders, and amber eyes sparkle with a familiar warmth.

It can't be possible, yet there she is—my mother, alive and vibrant after twenty years of absence.

A lump forms in my throat as I struggle to comprehend the impossible sight before me. How can she be here, at this moment, as if plucked from the depths of my memories and brought to life once more?

Questions swirl in my mind, but for now, only one thing matters—reaching out to the woman who has been lost to me for so long.

With trembling hands, I push open the creaky door and step outside, my heart pounding in my ears. Each step over the newly sprouted grass feels like an eternity as I cross the threshold, my eyes never leaving the figure beneath the tree. The distance between us closes with agonizing slowness, every moment stretching out into eternity while the season changes around us.

It's spring—warm yet cold and overstimulating colorful. The

light breeze carries the smell of fresh blossoms into my nose.

Finally, I stand before my mother, my breath catching in my throat as I struggle to find the words to speak. Time seems to stand still as our eyes meet.

And then, with a voice choked with emotion, I whisper her name. "Mom?"

For a moment, there's only silence, the air heavy with the weight of years gone by. And then, as if breaking free from a spell, my mother turns to face me, her eyes widening in disbelief. Recognition dawns in those familiar amber depths, followed by a flood of emotion that mirrors mine.

"Carena," she whispers, reaching for my hands. "You're here."

Under the spreading branches of a majestic tree, I look at my mother with tear-filled eyes. "I miss you," I whisper, my voice barely more than a breath against the stillness surrounding us. "Since you've been gone, it feels like a part of me is missing, too."

My mother, radiating warmth and tenderness, reaches out and envelops me in a comforting embrace, and I lean into her. She's here. I can feel her. I can smell her perfume, a sweet note of ylang-ylang.

"Oh, my sweetheart," she murmurs, caressing my hair. "You've grown into such a beautiful young woman. I've watched over you every step of the way, and though I may not be with you in body, my love for you knows no bounds."

Tears well in my eyes as I bury my face in my mother's shoulder, my heart aching with the bittersweetness of being able to feel her again. "I miss you so much," I whisper again, my voice choking with emotion. "I wish you were still here with us."

She holds me close, her touch a gentle reminder of the love that binds us together across the divide between life and death. "I miss you too, my sweet girl," she breathes, tenderly kissing my forehead. "But I'm happy where I am, and I want you to be happy too. Life is precious and fleeting, and we must cherish every moment."

As we stand beneath the tree, the season shifts again, and now summer envelops us in its warmth, the sun casting long shadows across the verdant landscape.

But as the light grows dimmer and the air colder, my mother's gaze turns wistful. My heart feels heavy knowing that our time together is drawing to a close. "My sweetheart," she says softly, her voice tinged with sadness. "As much as I wish I could stay with you forever, my time here is limited. Winter is approaching, and with it, I must return to where I belong."

She belongs to me, to our family.

The urge to grab her hand and pull her into the house to get more time with her rages through my mind. I can make this work. I can find a way to hide her and keep her with me!

The soft giggle of the playful children catches my attention. I don't have to look at them to know that it's us—Atlas, Adde, and

I.

In my mother's perfect world, she's outside, playing with us carefree. There's no sadness, death, and no cloud casting dark shadows over us.

My heart clenches at the thought of losing my mother once more, but I know I can't hold her back. No one knows how long she has been living with her aneurysm. It could have been hours, days, or weeks.

"I understand," I whisper, my voice trembling with emotion. "But please, promise me you'll always be watching over us, that you'll always be with me, even when I can't see you."

My mother smiles, her eyes shining with love and pride. "I promise, my sweetheart," she says, her voice a gentle breeze in the stillness of winter approaching. "I will always be with you, guiding, protecting, and loving you with all my heart. Always."

With one final embrace, we linger beneath the tree, our hearts intertwined in a love that transcends the boundaries of mortality. And as the first snowflakes drift down from the heavens, my mother's form begins to fade, her presence growing fainter with each passing moment.

"You might not be able to take this dream with you," my mother says, her voice fading, "but I want you to know I'm incredibly proud of you."

TWENTY-SIX

As the first rays of dawn filter through the curtains, I stir from my slumber, the remnants of sleep clinging to me like a comforting blanket. But before I can fully awaken, a heavy arm curls around my waist, pulling me close in a tender embrace.

While my senses are still clouded with drowsiness, I instinctively lean into the warmth of the man behind me, his presence a comforting anchor amidst the morning haze. I feel his breath against my neck, a gentle whisper against my skin that sends shivers of awareness coursing through my veins.

"Carena, I'm sorry," his voice murmurs softly, tinged with remorse. "I know I acted like a fool the last few days. I didn't mean to upset you."

Without uttering a word, I reach out, my hand finding his in the dim light of the early morning. Our fingers intertwine effortlessly, fitting together like puzzle pieces, a silent reassurance of the familiarity between us.

In that moment, words seem superfluous, unnecessary in the quiet intimacy of our shared moment. There's a comfort in the silence, a solace in the simple act of being together, wrapped in each other's arms.

With a contented sigh, I nestle closer to him, feeling the steady rhythm of his heartbeat beneath my ear. His warmth seeps into my bones, melting away the lingering chill of the night and filling me with a sense of peace that I haven't felt in a long time.

As I drift back into the depths of sleep, I feel a smile tugging at the corners of my lips, a reflection of the contentment that fills my heart.

In his arms, I find a refuge from the chaos of the outside world.

And as we lay there entwined in each other's arms, the soft light of dawn casting a gentle glow over us, I know I have found where I belong.

TWENTY-SEVEN

I stir from my slumber, the remnants of my dream still lingering in my mind like wisps of smoke. In the dream, I was enveloped in the warm embrace of a man, his arms wrapping around me with a tenderness that felt achingly real.

That's enough of a reminder that I need to get out of here. Knowing that my unconsciousness is aware of what's brewing inside me and using it against me in my most vulnerable state scares me.

As I shift in bed, my heart pounds with confusion when I feel the weight of an arm draped across my waist, anchoring me to reality with a jolt.

My breath catches in my throat as I realize it wasn't a dream at all—there *is* a man lying beside me, his presence a stark reminder of the blurred lines between fantasy and reality.

Panic surges through my veins like wildfire, my mind racing with a thousand questions and doubts.

Who is this man?

How did he end up in my bed?

And most importantly, what does his presence mean for my carefully guarded sense of independence?

Before I can process the whirlwind of emotions swirling inside me, the man stirs, his voice thick with sleep as he murmurs an apology. "I'm sorry again, Carena," he whispers, his words a balm to my frayed nerves. "I didn't mean to intrude, but you fell asleep, and I couldn't resist staying."

My heart clenches.

How could I let this happen?

As he reaches out to touch me, my body goes rigid with tension, my instincts screaming at me to flee. With a hastily muttered excuse, I scramble out of bed, my movements frantic as I rush to the bathroom's safety.

Alone in the small confines, I take a moment to catch my breath, my hands trembling as I splash cold water on my face. I stare at my reflection in the mirror, my eyes wide with disbelief at the surreal turn my morning has taken.

But there's no time to dwell on the unsettling find—I need to get out of here, now!

With a steely resolve, I get dressed, my movements fueled by a desperate need to escape.

As I storm out of the cabin into the biting cold of the morning, I don't stop when I hear my bedroom door open behind me. Without a coat, I stomp through the slush to my rental, but when I see that the road is still invisible beneath three feet of snow, I divert my aim to the next cabin in sight.

If I'm correct, Atlas and his family are staying there.

A high-pitched squeal of delight interrupts my frantic thoughts, followed by the pitter-patter of tiny feet after I knock on the door. The panic that settled in my bones eases when I'm greeted by the sight of my brother's energetic four-year-old daughter. With her golden curls bouncing and a mischievous sparkle in her eyes, Emily rushes forward to envelop my leg in a tight hug, her infectious laughter filling the air. For a moment, all thoughts of my dream—and reality—fade into the background as I lose myself in the warmth of my niece's embrace.

"I told you to stop opening the door," Atlas yells from the other room, and it only takes a heartbeat before he storms in our direction, his hands outstretched to grab Emily. He freezes when he sees me. "Oh, hi. I thought Emily tried to escape again to play in the snow," he says with a burst of nervous laughter.

"I don't want to intrude, but I need a place to stay," I say, bending down to pick up Emily.

As I wrap my arms around her, her heavy—yet light—weight tugs on an instinct I know all too well. It's the motherly instinct I felt for my siblings the day my mother died. Every fiber in my body tells me to hold on to her, to keep her safe from the rest of the world.

"Emily, go to Mama," Atlas says, lifting her out of my arms. "Remember the puzzle we started yesterday? I think it's time for you to finish it."

Emily pushes her lower lip out. "But, Dad. It's so hard."

"You got this," he replies, kissing her forehead before putting her on the ground.

"I'll try," Emily says, her vicious smile returning.

When Emily rounds the corner to reach the other room, Atlas closes the door behind me and points at the couch beside the crackling fireplace. "What's going on?"

My eyes land on the couch that looks the same as the one in my cabin. Without having control, my mind throws me back to Evander walking naked in my direction, and it forces me to walk over to a single chair in the corner.

"Did he hurt you?" Atlas asks after I don't answer. "Do you need me to throw him out?"

"Leon?"

Atlas' face is stone cold as he takes me in. "No, Evander."

My mouth pops open, but I shut it immediately. His guess isn't far off. I fled my cabin because of Evander, but not because he did something wrong.

I'm the problem.

The thought of Atlas thinking that Evander could be capable of hurting a fly breaks my heart.

"I can't help you if you don't talk to me, Carena," Atlas says, his brows drawing together.

I tilt my head. "What makes you think Evander hurt me?"

"I know my sister," he replies, sitting down on the couch. "I've been watching you run like a bear is chasing you since we were little."

"What are you trying to say?"

"You can't keep bolting away from people because they mean something to you."

I square my shoulders. "That's not true. Whatever you think you know about me is wrong."

Atlas clicks his tongue. "I know why Leon and you broke up."

I huff. "Is that so?"

"You got cold feet."

My heart pounds so loud in my chest I can hear my blood in my ears. "Is that what he told you?"

"Don't make the same mistake twice," he whispers, shaking his head.

I throw my hands in the air. "You know what? It was a bad idea to come here."

"Don't blow me off like that again," Atlas says, jumping to his feet.

Where does this come from?

I'm used to butting heads with Adde. But Atlas? He's the baby of the family, always supportive and unnaturally calm.

"Okay. You want to talk? Let's talk," I snarl, biting my lower lip. "I didn't get cold feet, he did. One morning, I woke up, and he was gone. He left me without saying a word, without an explanation, or regard what it would do to me."

"Carena," Atlas whispers, his eyes glued to me. "I didn't—"

"Oh, I'm not done yet," I say, pointing to the couch for him to sit down. "Since you're so interested in trying to understand me without asking questions. I'm running because I'm terrified of getting attached to someone else I'll eventually lose. Staying away from people makes it impossible to miss them."

"You can't seriously believe that?"

"I do. What I can't believe is that everyone always assumes they know me. Do you know how hard it was to raise you and Adde while watching our father wither away? No, you don't remember that part. You were only three years old when she died. For years, I busted my ass to make up for her absence. I sacrificed my childhood to ensure you have everything you need to thrive."

"No one expected that of you. You were a child, Carena."

"That doesn't change the fact that he couldn't function without her."

I let out a guttural exhale.

"I miss her, too," Atlas says, tears stinging in his eyes. "Yes, I don't remember her. I don't know how her voice sounded or how it felt when she tucked me in. I don't have a single memory of her, and it hurts. But that won't stop me from making every day worth living. Life goes on, and you should, too."

I can't move on—not after what I've done.

"Do you want to know the last words I said to her?" My throat burns, making it almost impossible to get the following words out. "I told her she's the worst mom because she wouldn't let me sleep in her bed."

My mind throws me back to the night I've been fighting to forget for twenty years. I remember her sweet face and amber eyes looking down at me as she told me she wasn't feeling well. She told me she didn't want to get me sick with whatever she had.

"If I had been there, if she had let me sleep with her, I could have been there to save her."

"Carena!" Atlas yells, storming in my direction. I cringe away when he grabs my hands, but he's stronger. "It wasn't your fault! There's nothing you could have done. You have to let her go. It's ruining you."

How can he say that? How can he demand that I forget our mother, the person who birthed us, the woman who gave everything to see us happy?

"You know what my biggest regret is?" Atlas asks, his voice thick with emotion. "That I lost my sister that day."

I hold my breath and look into his eyes.

"All I wanted was for you to take me by the hand and play with me. But you were too busy trying to fill shoes that were too big for you. And don't get me wrong. There's not a single day I'm not thankful for the strength you showed us and every cut and bruise you kissed. I can never repay you for what you did for me. But it's time for you to stop pleasing everyone and live."

I don't know how many more gut-punches I can take. This fucking hurts so much, I want to roll into a ball and cry.

"I don't know how you went from being the center of the family to totally abandoning us, but I need you to come back," he continues. "Not as our mother, but as a sister, as an aunt, and as the person I needed the most when we were little."

My thoughts are scattered, and my throat filled with a lump I can't swallow. "I'll do better. I promise," I croak out, still rummaging through everything he just said.

"You said that before, and look where we are now. It's okay if reintegrating into the family isn't your thing, but if you do, I need actions, not words."

I never thought about what it must have felt like for Atlas to have me hovering around him, trying to make up for the missing motherly component. It took some time to memorize everyone's schedules, to prepare three meals—well, noodles and sandwiches—for everyone, and to get Dad out to buy groceries.

I became his personal assistant without even realizing it.

"Emily would love to see you more often," Atlas adds, and the knife made of words he rammed into my chest just moments ago finally pierces my heart. "And so would Olivia and I."

What the fuck am I supposed to say now? How can I show him I want to change?

"Since we're still snowed in, could I spend some time with you guys?" I ask, swallowing over and over again to clear my throat. At this point, I'm unsure if I'm trying to stay because I still don't want to face Evander, or because I want to let actions speak.

"How would you feel taking Emily back to your place for a while?" he asks, massaging his neck. "Olivia and I could use some sleep."

Sleep, huh?

"I would love to take her," I reply as I feel a part of my heart stitching itself back together.

TWENTY-EIGHT

As the heavy wooden door creaks open, I step into the cozy cabin, my arms wrapped protectively around Emily. The warmth of the fire crackling in the stone fireplace greets us. I glance around uncertainly, feeling a bit out of my element with a child in tow, and I'm relieved to find my bedroom door closed.

What am I supposed to do with her?

I was so eager to show my brother that I'm a woman of action and want to become a bigger part of Emily's life that I forgot to consider what I'd do with her.

I've done this before—taken care of Atlas and Adde when they were almost her age—but I can't remember what I did to keep them happy. And even if I did, my cabin isn't designed to entertain a child.

Emily, however, brims with excitement, her eyes wide with wonder as she takes in the shelves lined with books of all shapes and sizes as I take her into the library, far away from the fire and

Evander. "Auntie, look at all the books!" she exclaims, tugging at my hand eagerly.

Smiling down at the little girl, I try to suppress my nerves. I agreed to look after Emily for a while, but I didn't anticipate how challenging it would be to entertain her with no toys. I'm used to my quiet, solitary life, and the prospect of being responsible for a lively four-year-old is daunting, to say the least.

"What do you usually play with?" I ask, cringing. I should know the answer. As her aunt, I should know what she likes, her favorite color, and which toys she can't live without.

"I don't know," she replies, shrugging her shoulders as she skips through the aisle.

I watch as her eyes light up with delight at the sight of a small table set up with pots of colorful markers to annotate books and stacks of paper.

"Can we paint, Auntie?" she asks eagerly, her fingers itching to dive into the vibrant hues.

I hesitate momentarily, unsure of my artistic abilities, but seeing the excitement in her eyes, I can't refuse. "Of course, cutie pie," I smile, guiding her over to the table. "Let's draw some beautiful pictures together."

As Emily uncaps the blue marker and begins to create swirling patterns on the paper, I find myself surprisingly relaxed. Emily's little voice fills the room as she talks about her art, banishing any lingering doubts from my mind. Together, we paint scenes of imaginary worlds where dragons soar through the sky, and unicorns dance among the stars.

This is so much easier than I expected. Emily doesn't need more than a few colors and paper, and she's ready to paint her day away without regard for the time.

Lost in our creative reverie, we weave stories to accompany our paintings, spinning tales of daring adventures and magical encounters. I marvel at my niece's vivid imagination, my worries melting away in the warmth of her innocent joy.

I remember when I used to make up creatures, map out new worlds, and talk to imaginary fairies that seemed so natural to me. And now that I've met Evander, maybe they were real. Perhaps the imagination of an adult isn't capable of producing such otherworldly beauty, and therefore, only children are allowed to dream of unimaginable things.

As we paint and laugh, unaware of the time, a figure appears in the doorway, watching us with a curious expression. It's Evander, tall and handsome, with a mischievous twinkle in his eye.

"Having fun, are we?" he asks, his voice laced with amusement.

I startle at the sound of his voice, suddenly self-conscious in his presence. I've forgotten that we aren't alone in the cabin, lost in the world of colors and fairy tales.

Emily, however, greets the newcomer with a beaming smile.

"Come join us!" she exclaims, reaching out to him with paint-stained hands.

Evander hesitates for a moment, glancing between Emily and me. But then, with a shrug and a grin, he steps into the room, closing the door behind him.

"Well, since you asked so nicely," he says, striding over to the table and picking up a marker. "But I warn you, I'm not very good at this."

I watch in bemusement as Evander uncaps the marker and sketches a rough outline on his paper. Despite his protestations, I can't help but admire the calm confidence with which he wields the marker, his movements fluid and sure.

As he continues, I can't shake the feeling that there's something different about him. There's a spark of something in his eyes, a hint of magic that lingers in the air.

And then, suddenly, it all becomes clear.

Evander leans close to Emily with a mischievous grin and whispers something in her ear. The little girl's eyes widen in surprise, and then she bursts into giggles.

"What did you say?" I ask, panic gripping me.

Evander leans back with a sly grin, his eyes twinkling with mischief. "Ah, now that would be snitching," he says, wagging a finger playfully. "But let's just say, if Emily promises not to tell anyone my secret, I might just have a little surprise for her."

The little girl's eyes light up excitedly, and she nods eagerly. "I promise! I won't tell anyone!"

With a wink, Evander raises his hands and closes his eyes, a look of intense concentration on his face. And then, in a flash of light and color, the entire room shifts and transforms around us. The shelves of books vanish, replaced by towering easels and tables piled high with paint and brushes. The walls shimmer and dance with vibrant hues, as if alive with the energy of creativity.

I gasp, hardly daring to believe my eyes. I glance at Emily, who squeals with delight as she darts around the room, exploring every nook and cranny of the newly transformed art studio.

"You can't trust her to keep a secret like that," I say, my hands getting sweaty from the position he put me in.

"You kept me a secret for twenty years," Evander replies, smirking at me. "What's the difference?"

"I was ten. She's four. The first thing she'll tell Atlas is that you have magic."

He shrugs his shoulders. "And I do."

"Evander. This is going too far. This could ruin everything."

"You need to learn that not everything is in your control. Plus, I trust her. Just look at her."

My gaze falls back on Emily, who is elbow-deep in a bucket of green paint.

"You might have outgrown your childhood, but this is your chance to relive it," he says, walking over to Emily, pushing his hand into another bucket, and throwing red paint at me.

It hits me straight on.

I gasp in shock, holding my arms out wide to inspect the damage. "No, you didn't," I snarl, my eyes falling onto another bucket filled with purple.

"What are you going to do about it?" Evander laughs, and Emily joins him with a high-pitched squeal when she sees me.

The first splash of paint I throw at him is fueled by pure rage.

How dare he ruin my outfit!

The second and the third slowly turn into something I haven't felt in years—fun.

Soon, Emily joins us, and as I watch my niece's eyes light up with wonder, I can't help but feel a sense of gratitude towards Evander. In the space of a few short minutes, he has done more for Emily than I ever have. Eventually, Emily will forget about it.

But I won't.

As the evening wears on and the sun dips below the horizon, casting long shadows across the cabin, I notice Emily's boundless energy beginning to wane. The little girl's laughter softens into gentle giggles, and her movements become slower, more deliberate. Sensing that Emily is growing tired, I glance at the clock on the wall and realize it's getting late.

Instead of whisking her back to my brother's cabin as initially planned, a thought occurs to me: why not let her stay the night?

Atlas would have come for her if he were concerned or wanted her back. But he isn't here.

With a smile, I turn to my niece. "How about you stay with me tonight, cutie pie?" I suggest gently. "We can have a sleepover and paint our nails before bed. What do you say?"

The little girl perks back up for a moment. "Yes, please!" Emily exclaims, clapping her hands together with delight. "Is he going to join us?" she asks, pointing at Evander.

I smile at her. "Is that what you want?"

"Yes! Yes!"

And so we settle in for an impromptu sleepover. We rummage through a collection of nail polish Evander summoned for us, selecting bright, cheerful colors to adorn our fingertips. As we paint each other's nails, I marvel at the innocence and simplicity of the moment, the joy of sharing something as simple as a bottle of nail polish with Emily.

Occasionally, I look down at Evander sitting on the ground. He watches Emily's little fingers tremble as she struggles to aim for my nails.

As we finish up, she lets out a soft yawn, her eyelids growing heavy with sleep. I smile affectionately, testing the dryness of her nails one last time before I scoop her up into my arms. Gently tucking her beneath the covers, I settle down beside her, wrapping my arms around the small, warm bundle of energy.

"Do you want me to tell you a story before you go to sleep?" I ask softly, brushing a stray lock of hair away from her forehead.

The little girl nods eagerly, her eyes bright with anticipation. "Yes, please, Auntie! Tell me a story!"

And so, I weave a tale of my childhood, of adventures shared with my brother on lazy summer afternoons. I recount the time we built a fort in the backyard, using only old blankets and cardboard boxes, and the time we went on a treasure hunt in search of buried treasure.

I watch Emily's eyelids grow heavier and heavier, her breathing slowing to a steady rhythm. And then, with a contented sigh, she nestles closer against my side, her small hand clutching my shirt tightly.

With a tender smile, I gently kiss her forehead, whispering a silent promise to always be there for her, protect her, and love her no matter what. And as I watch her drift off into peaceful slumber, a wave of pure joy washes over me.

I didn't know what to expect when I received the wedding invitation months ago. But running into my ex with a fake boyfriend as my plus-one, reliving my failed engagement, having the best sex of my life, and coming clean with Atlas wasn't on my mind when I accepted it.

"Do you think we can leave tomorrow?" I whisper, locking eyes with Evander.

"I'm certain," he replies, and my heart sinks.

He cocks his head. "Isn't that the answer you wanted?"

"It is. It's just that I'm going to miss this," I reply, pressing my cheek against Emily's head. "I forgot how it feels to be carefree," I add, curling one of Emily's locks around my finger.

"I'm happy for you," Evander says, smiling at me. "Moments like this are what life is all about."

TWENTY-NINE

"What happened to her?" I ask, gently caressing Emily's cheek as she curls into my chest.

Evander's smile slips as I change the topic without warning.

I told myself I wouldn't ask, but since our time together is running out, I can't suppress my curiosity any longer.

"I thought we were destined to be together," Evander replies, knowing exactly to whom I'm referring to.

"But?"

He sniffs through his nose. "I wasn't as fortunate to grow up in a house where free will was acceptable. From a young age, I had to help on our farm so my father could bring enough food to the table. The work didn't bother me. On the contrary, I loved helping out. And that's how I met her, Alia. She was gorgeous from the inside out. But she was marked for someone else since she was born."

The way his voice shifts as he talks about Alia makes me feel the heartbreak he's going through.

"Young people in love are stupid. We thought we could outrun our responsibilities, and we did…for two days." He exhales sharply. "They found us."

My heart screams at me to stop his suffering, to tell him it's okay, to stop the story there.

But I don't.

"After we were dragged back to our village, I was exiled. Alone and without money, I wandered until my legs couldn't take another step. By losing Alia and the ability to return home, I lost everything."

He lets out another sniffing sound, followed by a chuckle. "And then there was this man. He approached me and promised me he could make me the most powerful man in the universe. He promised I could make every dream come true. And I believed him." He shakes his head. "I didn't ask for any details. I didn't even read the contract I signed because I was so desperate to get back home, back to Alia."

My stomach turns when I realize where his story is going.

"When I lifted the pen off the paper, I could feel it. Strength, wisdom, ultimate power. I ran back to Alia as fast as my legs could carry me." He exhales sharply as he presses his hair out of his face. "I'll never forget the confusion when I looked into her eyes. She didn't know who I was, and no matter what I tried, I couldn't make her remember. And then, I felt the tugging on my being when I was summoned back to that man. All he had to do was rub that little lamp he bound me to, and I would appear."

My gaze shifts to the shiny golden lamp in my suitcase.

"What happened next?" I ask, taking in the intricate carvings of his *home*.

"He sold me to the highest bidder. And for years, I served my new master, doing unspeakable things. It wasn't until I realized I might be bound to the lamp and an owner, but I could limit my wishes. After he realized I wasn't of any use anymore, I was sold again. This went on and on until one day, my newest owner grew tired of me and tossed my lamp into the ocean. He wanted to ensure that I can't grant any more wishes."

"I'm so sorry, Evander. I can't imagine what that must have felt like," I say, guilt gnawing on me.

I'm not better than any of those men.

I've used him. I abused his power by demanding more and more with every wish.

"Ask your next question," Evander says, eyeing me wearily.

"How did you end up in my grandma's attic?" I ask, closing my eyes.

"She found me, or rather, my lamp," he replies. "When I washed up on shore, she grabbed and cleaned my lamp. You know what she said when she saw me for the first time?" Evander chuckles, and the sudden shift in his demeanor catches me off guard. "She told me I look like I've seen better days."

"That sounds about right," I answer, seeing my grandma's face before my eyes as she studies him.

"Do you want to know her first wish?" he asks, sitting down on the bed beside Emily.

I nod slowly.

"She never made one," he says, smacking his lips. "She told me that there's nothing I can give her she can't get herself."

"When did she…you know…find you?" I ask, my brain trying to connect the dots.

"Long before you were born," Evander says, and I can see in his eyes that he knows where I'm going with this. "Now you're probably wondering why she didn't use me to save her own child. If I've learned one thing over the years I was bound to your grandmother, it's that the universe works in mysterious ways. She believed everything happens for a reason, and even though I begged her to let me help, she declined."

"No," I whisper, my body stiffening.

That doesn't make any sense.

My grandma would have done everything she could to bring her only daughter back. I know it.

"So, you could have helped her?" I ask as panic claws at my chest.

"I can't say for certain. But I would have tried if she had let me."

Knowing that there was a possibility that my mother could

still be alive hurts so damn much.

"Why didn't you do anything?" I almost choke on my words. "If you were there and could have prevented her death, why didn't you go against my grandma's wishes?"

"I tried, but without a wish, my hands were tied. The only thing I could control was staying with you after you found me. I tried to help you."

"All this time, you stuck around because you pitied me?"

"No," he replies hastily. "I know it hurts to hear what I have to say, but don't twist my words."

How can I believe him? There are always two sides to a story. So what if he's telling me all of this to plead his innocence, framing my grandma, who isn't here to defend herself?

"I think it's time for bed," I say, pulling the blankets over Emily.

"Please don't shut me out again," Evander says, closing his eyes to take a deep breath.

"I-I just need a minute to straighten my thoughts," I lie, my eyes glued to Emily.

"I'm sorry," Evander whispers as he stands up and walks to the door. "But I had to tell you. Now you know."

Know what?

That my grandma accepted my mother's fate?

That Evander might have been able to help her?

No matter how I twist and turn the facts, something isn't

adding up, and this long-ass weekend needs to be over because my heart can't take it anymore.

THIRTY

I stretch and yawn, blinking away the remnants of sleep as I sit up in bed. Moments later, I hear the sound of footsteps approaching, and my heart skips a beat as the door swings open to reveal my brother, his wife, my sister, and our father standing in the doorway, their arms laden with trays of steaming breakfast dishes.

"Good morning, sleepyhead!" my brother exclaims, his voice filled with warmth and the energy of a man who either had a good night's rest or the best night of his life—childless. "We brought breakfast!"

With a squeal, Emily leaps out of bed and runs into her father's arms, her face beaming with joy. "Daddy!" she cries, wrapping her tiny arms around his neck tightly as he picks her up. "We had so much fun last night! Can we do it again?"

Atlas chuckles and ruffles her hair affectionately. "We'll see," he says with a smile. "But for now, let's enjoy breakfast together."

"Poor Evander had to sleep on the couch last night," Olivia says, pressing her lips into a thin line. "Believe me when I tell you, no bed is big enough for two adults and a child. But thank you so much for taking her. It looks like she had a blast."

I want to make a comment about them leaving Emily in my hands for such a long time, but I don't because I genuinely enjoyed her company.

"It was alright," Evander says, stepping through the bathroom door into my room. "I don't mind sleeping on the couch."

This conversation would have been different if someone had caught him outside my bed if Emily wasn't there. I've never experienced it myself, but I know that couch sleeping is the slow death of most relationships.

"What are you guys doing here?" I ask, immediately regretting my tone, but it feels too much like an ambush.

"We wanted to spare you seeing Leon again. I'm really sorry," Adde says, her hands trembling with anger. "If I had known what he did to you, I would have never invited him. Why didn't you say something?"

And...here we go again.

Of course, Atlas told Adde what I said yesterday. Hopefully, it was far away from Aunt Margaret's ears because otherwise, everyone and their cat will know.

Ugh.

Why am I still protecting him? He left me; he threatened me.

He deserves what's coming his way.

"How about we mark today as a fresh start?" Evander cuts in, grabbing the dishes out of my sister's hand.

Adde grunts, overthinking his words. She loves drama so much that I don't know if she will accept his offer.

"We can't let him get away with this, though," Olivia says, staring at me.

Somebody woke up on the wrong foot, choosing violence.

"Revenge. Now that's something I can get behind," Evander replies, steering towards the small table beside the fireplace. "What do you have in mind?"

"You're going to stay out of this," I exclaim, jumping out of bed. "You've done enough."

"Not enough for my taste," Evander replies, and my body stiffens when his eyes wander over me. I can't control the heat rushing into my face as he sizes me up like I'm his next meal.

"There's a child present," my father warns, claiming his spot on the couch. "To change the subject, I need to tell you something."

The tone of his voice indicates that it's something serious. Immediately, my body reacts to the tension.

"What is it?" I ask, hastily sitting down beside him. "Are you sick?"

"No," he laughs, waiting for everyone to gather around the

table. "I...met someone."

The room falls silent enough that I can hear the fire crackle. I look around the room, searching for someone to step forward, and ask the burning question on my tongue.

When no one does, I do. "A woman?"

He nods, and the knot in my stomach unties when I see his features soften. "Yes, a woman. She used to be good friends with your mother. I stumbled upon her in my support group."

"Who is she?" Adde asks, sitting at the edge of the couch to look past me.

"Jane. I don't know if you remember her, but her husband passed away two years ago."

Jane. Jane?

No, it doesn't ring any bells.

But does it matter who she is?

He has been alone for twenty years, and the last time I saw this look on his face was because of our mother. If Jane makes him glow, I need to support him.

"I'm so happy for you," I say, linking my arm into his and leaning against his shoulder.

My father presses his hand against mine, chuckling softly. "I was terrified to tell you guys. I wasn't sure how you all would react."

"Because of mom?" Atlas asks, cocking his head. "I can't speak for all of us, but I've been waiting for the day you put yourself out there again. We all know that no one can replace our mom, but you're too young to stay alone."

It never crossed my mind that our father would eventually meet a new woman—in his case, an old friend. While I try to find something that feels unsettling about it, nothing comes up. And even if I had concerns, I'm not responsible for him anymore.

"When are we going to meet her?" Adde asks, a smile curving her lips.

"It's not official yet, but when the time comes, I would love for you to come over for dinner to meet her," he replies, his cheeks turning rosy.

"This is huge," I say, squeezing his arm one more time before my eyes fall on Evander, who has been observing us without saying a word. The smile he gives me warms my heart, and it feels like this has been the moment he has been waiting for.

Twenty years of guilt, tension, and frustration wash away as I lean into my father, his excitement for a new beginning rubbing off on me. I've been waiting for silent permission to move on, and until now, I didn't know it was linked to him.

I know if he's okay, so will I.

If he can move on from the biggest heartbreak he'll ever experience, so can I.

"You probably can't wait to go home," Olivia says, looking at me. "I'm surprised you got a few days off. You're always so busy."

"Owning a business will do that to you," I answer, trying not to think of all the work waiting for me once I land. "It didn't help that there is barely any reception up here."

Atlas chuckles. "Then you're lucky. I couldn't even call off work. They probably think I'm dead."

"That's not funny," Olivia says, swatting his arm. "You told me you notified them."

He shrugs his shoulders. "Well, I did, but neither the email nor the text messages went out. I didn't want to freak you out because there's nothing we can do to change our situation."

I admire my brother's enthusiasm. No matter what life throws at him, he just keeps going with a smile on his face. Potentially losing a job would freak any person out, but not him. If push comes to shove, he'll go out and find a new job with a smile on his face.

"When I grow up, I want to be you," I laugh, sitting up straight.

The room breaks out in laughter, and a sense of peace settles over me. For the first time in twenty years, I'm surrounded by my family in a warm and comfortable room. I watch as Adde and Atlas exchange playful banter, their laughter filling the air with something I haven't heard in a while. Our father keeps to himself, his happiness radiating out of him like a catalyst.

As we eat, I savor each moment, knowing that once we're finished, it will be time for me to say *see you later*. Once we're done, everyone will return to their lives without looking back.

I try to stretch out the breakfast as long as possible, but eventually, the meal comes to an end, and my heart sinks as I realize that the time has come to part ways. I glance over at Evander, feeling a pang of sadness at the thought of letting him go.

Atlas notices my somber expression and reaches out to squeeze my hand reassuringly. "Don't worry, sis," he says softly. "We'll see each other again soon."

With a heavy heart, I nod, trying to blink back the tears that threaten to spill over. I know this weekend was a shit show for me, but I'll still cherish this memory—all of us in one room— the laughter and love shared, and the sense of belonging I've longed for for so many years.

"It's time," my father says, gathering the empty plates. "I'll stay behind with Adde and River to clean up, but you should go to catch the next flight."

"Where is River?" I ask, just realizing that he isn't here.

"He's fine," Atlas cuts in, swatting his hand. "Apparently, he thought he was invincible and drained an entire wine bottle on a dare. Needless to say, the wine won."

I chuckle, wishing I could have been there to see it.

"It's time," my father says, piling up the empty dishes.

I don't want to go. If there's an option to stay longer, I would take it, but I know everyone is getting ready to leave.

"Let me grab my things," I reply, motioning to Evander to do the same.

It takes me less than ten minutes to gather my few things, and I halt when my eyes catch a glimpse of Evander's lamp. I bend down, caressing the cold metal with my finger as sadness slams into me.

I knew it.

I knew my heart would cave, and I know the exact moment it decided to thump faster when Evander was around. Not only has my vagina decided to jump ships, but now my heart is battling against the crippling anxiety of my departure.

As I prepare to leave the cabin behind, my suitcase in Evander's arms, I take one last look around the room, etching the image of my family gathered together in my mind, a reminder of the love that sustained me through the years. Everything I did for my family has finally paid off, and it's my time to leave that chapter behind and concentrate on what's important—myself.

THIRTY-ONE

If saying *see you later* to my family wasn't hard enough, it's time to rip off the bandaid that's really going to hurt.

"Thank you for coming with me," I say to Evander as I flop into the driver's seat.

"You're welcome," he replies, waving at my family as they return to their cabins to prepare for their departure. "It's not like I had any say in it, though," he adds, and I cringe.

Way to take the wind out of my sails.

"I couldn't have done this without you," I continue, taking a deep breath to prepare myself for my following words. "But as much as I enjoyed your company, this can't continue."

Evander slowly lowers his hand, and I feel his eyes burning into my profile.

"What's your next step?" he asks as the tires crunch through the slush.

"We need to find a way to free you," I say, biting my lip. "I shouldn't have used you like this."

"You did nothing wrong. I enjoy helping you."

The urge to bang my head against the steering wheel pops into my head.

"But that's the thing," I reply, swallowing hard. "I want to know what I'm capable of by myself. Knowing you're in the background granting my every wish isn't normal. Plus, it's not fair to you."

"I thought we talked about this," he breathes, looking out the window as we round the corner and the cabins disappear behind a row of pine trees. "I chose to stay with you."

I scoff. "Because I am your new master."

"No, because doing something good for someone feels amazing."

So that's what I am to him: a chance to redeem himself.

"But I'm no longer a charity case. At some point, you'll realize that, and you'll choose to go. It's just a matter of time," I reply, my voice shaking. "It's easier to break things off now than wait another day."

"I'm never going to leave you," Evander says, exhaling sharply.

Another deep breath.

"Everyone does. Eventually, you—"

"No, I won't change my mind," he cuts in, his voice firm. "There's nothing you can do that will scare me away. I'm right where I'm supposed to be."

"Stop making this harder than it is," I say, shaking my head. "If you don't tell me how to release you, I'll find a way."

He huffs. "That's your choice."

"Aren't you sick of serving humans? Don't you want to live free?"

"I made my peace with it."

I grip the steering wheel harder to keep my emotions under control. "But I can't. This is wrong on so many levels. What's your end goal? Serving me until the day you die?"

"I can't die."

"That's even worse. I'm going to grow old and weak. And what are you going to do after I'm gone?"

Evander stares at me for a long time. "I can change my appearance if that's what is bothering you. We can make it work."

I let out a hysterical chuckle. "It's not about how you look. It's about how you got so used to being a servant that you forgot how it feels like to have your own mind. Whatever we had, how do I know it was something you wanted, or you just did it to make me happy? There's no way I can keep my wishes apart from what *you* truly want."

At this point, my hands are trembling, and I consider pulling over.

"I can differentiate between your needs and mine. But where is all of this coming from? I thought you enjoyed my company."

"I did, but I wish it weren't like this."

"Like what?"

Silence.

What am I supposed to say? What am I so scared of?

"That you're bound to me and have to listen to every word I say. That you're trapped in this continuous loop of serving one person after another. And that this between us can never become a reality because I can't promise you anything in return. Life is fragile and unpredictable. No human can make a promise without having the tiniest doubt in the back of their head that they might not be able to uphold it. I have nothing, *nothing*, to offer."

For a few minutes, we drive in silence.

I thought I knew what I wanted when I fought with the key to lock my house four days ago. It was supposed to be a simple weekend away, getting through my sister's wedding and returning to my mundane routine.

Who knew that four days are enough to shake your life up? The solid foundation on which I thought I had built my entire existence started crumbling the second I saw him. And from there on out, he kept hammering against that foundation, taking it piece by piece to build something new.

Does he know what he did to me? Does he realize how fast humans get attached to other people?

"What do you want, Carena?" Evander asks, breaking the

silence. "And don't lie to me. I can tell when you do."

Even if I wanted to lie, I no longer have the strength.

"In another life, I would say *you*. But I can't. I'll never know if any of your actions are because you want to please me or because I made you do them. I won't use you like that."

"You don't have to."

"Evander, please stop. You helped me get through this weekend. You gave me so much that will help me turn my life around, and there's only one thing I can give you in return. Your freedom. You deserve to be free."

"I won't accept it," Evander replies, crossing his arms.

"Then you don't leave me another choice." I clench my teeth.

Evander inhales deeply. "Then, wish for it, Darling. Say what you want."

I close my eyes. "I wish you were free and far away from here."

I take a deep breath before I open my eyes.

Evander is…still sitting beside me, arms crossed.

"Stop it. I know you can suppress my wishes. I'm just trying to help you," I wince, inhaling again to repeat my words.

He shakes his head slowly. "That's not true. I can't deny wishes. Some of your wishes, I granted because it was my duty. But some of them, you made come true by yourself."

"I've seen you deny wishes," I snarl, desperation clawing at my throat.

I need him gone. I need him out of my life *right now* because if he's not, I don't know if I can control myself any longer.

"Right before you sought me out," he says, his voice laced with sadness, "it was you who stopped believing in me. You can't throw a wish into the universe without believing in it."

"So, you're saying I'm the reason my key broke?"

"It wasn't me," he says, shrugging his shoulders.

"But I believe in you now, and I'm imagining it. I wish you were free," I repeat, this time not skipping a beat.

I look over at him, and for the first time since our paths crossed, he looks defeated.

"See, nothing happens," I point out, on the brink of tears. "Oh, shit. I still owe you a wish," I whisper, recognizing my error. "Just say it. What do you want from me?"

He looks at me, and I get uncomfortable with how long he holds my stare. "You really don't know, do you?"

My stomach twists. "Know what?"

"You granted my three wishes."

I shake my head, almost losing control over the Jeep. "No, I didn't. You still have a wish."

He grabs my hand and squeezes it. "Remember in the hot tub?"

"I really don't want to think about that right now," I say, my mind slowing down my sentence with each word.

He isn't talking about the sex.

242

When we were in the hot tub, he asked me what I see in my future. His next words drowned in the sounds of the water.

Damn it. I should have paid closer attention.

"I still don't understand," I mumble, lifting my shaking foot off the gas paddle.

"You told me your past, present, and future. And that's all I needed to help you realize what you have been running from most of your life."

Past—he wished to know what happened to my mother right before the ceremony started.

Present—he wished to know how I was feeling during our dance.

Future—he asked me what I see in my future.

This entire time, he had me granting his wishes, not to help him but to help me. He tried to make me realize what life is really about.

Nevertheless, it doesn't explain how he's able to dodge my newest wish since he's still bound to me.

"If we're even, why are you still here?"

"Because of your wish."

I'm so confused, my brain seizes.

I've made so many wishes over twenty years. There's no way I can keep track of them all, since my newest one can't be the one he's referring to.

When the car comes to a stop, I look at him. "What's

happening?"

"You said *you wish I wasn't bound to you* and that *I have to listen to every word you say.*"

I remember those words because I said them just a few minutes ago.

"Yeah, but—"

Oh my gosh.

"I didn't use it as a wish. I accidentally said *I wish* to start the sentence. I—"

His eyes bore into me. "Yet you meant it."

"I-I…no."

"But I do because those were the words that freed me."

My breath comes out in rapid huffs as I realize what I've done.

This is what I wanted. Setting him free so he can go on without me.

So why is my heart feeling like it's about to jump out of my chest? Why does the thought of losing him hurt so much?

Why can't I make up my fucking mind about what I want?

"What are you going to do next?" I ask, looking at him. My throat is as dry as the desert as I wait for his words.

He's free. He can go wherever he wants.

I study the handsome man before me.

He hasn't changed.

I don't know what I expected to happen once he isn't a djinn anymore, but that it does nothing to him surprises me.

"I'm free," he replies, shrugging his shoulders. "I'm not bound to a lamp anymore."

"But, how do *you* feel?"

"Pretty tired," he says, yawning.

That's it? That's how it feels when a djinn loses his power?

I gather all my strength to ask the next question, knowing his answer might not be what I want to hear. "So, what now?"

He shrugs his shoulders. "I guess you were right. It's my time to leave," he says, and I can practically hear my heart break.

I knew it.

Everything that happened between us was just him following orders. As much as I wanted this connection between us to be real, the moment our bond disappeared, he didn't have to play house anymore.

"Could you drive me to the next town?" he asks, leaning back to close his eyes.

I want to scratch his eyes out.

"Sure," I snarl, contemplating throwing his ass out of the Jeep, but that would go against everything I promised.

It was my wish to free him. He tried to warn me; if I had listened to him, I could have had everything I wanted.

And while it hurts knowing that everything he said and did was a fluke, I must remember why I did this: *it's my time to regain control of my own life and begin to live.*

Twenty minutes into our descent, I can hear Evander snoring lightly. I can't imagine what it must feel like to go from having magic to being a human. The urge to touch him one last time burns in my fingertips, and I bite my tongue to redirect the pain I'm feeling in my chest.

Eventually, we drive out of the park limits and I see a town in the distance. With every mile we approach it, I can feel a range of emotions wash over me.

Why do I have to be such a bitch? Why does everything always have to go my way?

"We're here," I say, hitting the brake hard enough for Evander's head to jolt forward because I can't bring myself to touch him.

"Well, thank you," he replies, rubbing the sleep out of his eyes as he looks around.

Silently, I study him as he takes our surroundings in. As requested, I drove him to where he wanted, parking in front of a cabin with a vacancy sign. My thoughts go rigid as I wait for him to say something, to change his mind.

I give him another minute to collect himself before clearing my throat when I realize his decision is final.

"Wait a second," I say, remembering something I should have done long ago. Hastily, I jump out of the Jeep, open the trunk, and grab something that no longer belongs to me.

"I'm really sorry," I say, walking over to the passenger door where Evander is waiting for me. I hold his lamp out. "Here."

His eyes linger on the lamp briefly before he looks at me. "I don't need it anymore," he says, shrugging his shoulders.

"But it's your *home*," I whisper.

"I want you to keep it," he replies, pushing the object in my direction without touching me.

"I can't keep it," I mumble, pressing it against his chest. "Please, don't do this to me."

He takes a step back. "This lamp holds so many memories. I can't take it with me, not where I'm going."

I shake my head slowly. Always these damn riddles. But I don't try to solve this one. I don't want to know where he's going because if I do, I'll always think about searching for him.

"Good luck, Evander," I say, holding back tears as I drop my outstretched hands, clinging to the lamp like it's a lifeline.

"I'm going to miss you, Darling," he says, lowering his head.

"I'm so sorry. I—"

"Stop apologizing," he says, smiling at me. "I can go wherever I want. I can grow old and listen to people's wishes without reacting to them. For the first time in centuries, I'm free."

I can barely breathe.

"I guess we both got what we wanted," I whisper, lowering my gaze.

"It's for the best," he replies, taking another step away from me.

THIRTY-TWO

My heart beats in my throat as I jump into the Jeep, fiddling with the key to start the motor.

This wasn't a freaking bandaid I had to rip off; it felt like ripping out my heart. How can my feelings be so strong for a person I just met?

For a minute, I debate what to do next and laugh. I don't have another option than going home and extinguishing the dumpster fire that is probably blazing at work. I'll return home and dive right back into what I do best: organizing chaos.

When I press on the gas paddle, I hear the back door being ripped open.

"What the fuck?" I yell as I slam on the brakes, ready to fight whoever has the guts to mess with me.

"You know what, I changed my mind," Evander says with a smile, jumping into the car. "I really thought you were going to run after me and confess your feelings, but I guess the joke is on me," he continues, leaning forward. "I thought the Darling part would get your blood boiling. But that's another point for you."

I've noticed he has been calling me Darling, and just as I expected, he used that name to ruffle my feathers.

"What are you doing?" I snarl, staring into his deep brown eyes.

He chuckles. "Isn't it obvious? I'm going with you."

"Stop playing with me and get out," I huff.

"You know what? No."

"This wasn't a request. It's a demand. Get out," I yell, pointing out the open door.

He wets his lips, and I know the next part will be gut-wrenching.

"I've watched over you for almost twenty years," he begins, his brows drawing together. "At first, I was an invisible friend who wanted to mend a little girl's heart after she lost her mother. You were so small, so innocent." He huffs. "Throughout your teenage years, it was quite entertaining supporting you through all your crazy dreams. Nevertheless, you needed a friend." He takes a long pause. "The first time I saw you happy and thought I wasn't needed anymore was when you went to college and started writing. I was so close to letting you go."

My heart pounds so loud in my chest that I can barely hear him. "Why didn't you?"

He looks at me like it's obvious. "You," he says, smiling at me. "You weren't that little child anymore I needed to protect. You outgrew me, and I realized that when you wished to ace a test and you didn't believe in your wish."

"So you couldn't grant it?" I reply, trying to figure out where his story is going.

"Precisely. From there on out, your wishes were half-hearted because you believed in yourself. You didn't need me."

"Why did you stick around then?" I ask again, feeling a wave of anger pulsing through me.

He huffs. "You're not listening."

"I am," I scoff.

He leans even closer, and I feel his breath caress my face when he speaks. "I fell in love with you."

The silence between us presses the air out of my lungs.

"That's not funny," I reply, my mouth as dry as the desert.

"Darling, I love you," he says, reaching for my hand.

This has to be a dream or a cruel trick. Maybe he realized when I was about to abandon him in a random town that he needed my help. Or perhaps he is more viscous than I thought and enjoys playing with me.

But what if what he says is true?

When our fingers touch, I feel a spark between us.

I don't care if this is a trap. If he wants to play dirty, so be it. I deserve it after what I've done to him.

He leans forward, closing his eyes.

I know where he's going with this, but a kiss won't be enough.

I slam the car into park, and before Evander can say another word, I crawl over the center consul towards him. My knee hits the seat as I fling myself at him, pressing him with my hands against the seat.

"You're a dick," I whisper through clenched teeth as I position my legs around his thighs. "I thought you were leaving."

"Never," Evander whispers into my mouth just before our lips collide.

I thought I learned what desperate sex feels like when he pushed his cock into me for the first time. I wanted him so badly and couldn't think straight.

But what I feel now is sheer desperation as I try to rip my pants off after I realize he can't help me undress in the blink of an eye anymore.

I don't want Evander; I need him. I need him more than air.

Within seconds—and a few bruises later since a car is not the ideal place to make up and get undressed—we're bare from the waist down.

"Slow down," he groans when I crawl onto his lap, pressing my chest against him to pin him between the seat and myself.

"Don't tell me what to do," I growl as I grab his dick to slide it between my folds.

His chuckle reverberates through my body as I lower myself onto him, my legs still sore from our steamy hot tub exercise.

"You're going to be the death of me," he moans as I rock my hips against him, teasing him with every movement.

He grabs my ass, lifting and dropping me at a pace that makes my pussy clench around him. Desperately, I lean forward, pressing my lips onto his before his tongue enters my mouth.

"You ask me what I see in my future," I moan after breaking our kiss. For a moment, he halts, and I feel his cock throbbing inside me, demanding more. "You," I whisper, staring into his eyes as I let myself down slowly on him, taking in his entire length to the hilt.

His breath becomes ragged, and I feel him coating my insides with his cum as he shatters at my words.

THIRTY-THREE

*Y*ou know what really sucks?

When you start traveling with a djinn, and now it's time to go back with a human.

I laugh hysterically when I see the sweat forming on Evander's face as he searches for his ID.

"Sir, I won't be able to provide you with a ticket without a valid ID," the man behind the counter says, his voice tinged with impatience.

"I know I have it…somewhere," Evander replies, checking his pockets for the fourth time. "I just need a minute."

Why didn't it cross my mind that everything he produced with his magic would vanish once he lost his power?

"Thank you for your help. We'll be right back," I say, grinning at him as I grab my ID off the counter and push Evander to the side, out of earshot. "You won't find it," I whisper, watching him turn every pocket inside out.

"It has to be on me. I know it," he says, ignoring my words.

My eyes scan the giant hall. "It's alright," I say, grabbing him by the shoulders. "Go and grab us some coffee," I add, handing him a twenty-dollar bill I always keep in my pants for emergencies like this one. "I'll be right back."

"You want me to *order* coffee?" he asks, holding the money away from him like it's poison.

"A vanilla latte, please," I grin, fishing my phone from my other pocket.

Evander mumbles under his breath as he looks around to find his destination.

I should go with him. I should grab him by his hand and stand beside him during his first step of relearning to be human, but I need to do something.

The phone only rings twice before Jinelle picks up.

"Good lord, Carena. Are you okay? I was worried sick about you," she says, and I hear the panic in her voice.

"I'm fine," I reply, following Evander to watch him tackle his first human task. "How is everything going?"

"The files you sent back to me are unusable. I'm unsure if it was the connection or the scanner you used, but I've been calling you at fifteen-minute intervals. Where were you?"

"I'm really sorry. We got snowed in and…"

"And what?"

"I need you to hold the fort for a few more days," I add,

sucking in a breath.

"What do you mean *a few more days*? Where are you?"

"I won't be able to fly back," I say, trying to keep the conversation as generic as possible.

"Why not?" Jinelle's shrill voice squeaks through the earpiece. "You can't just leave me. I don't know what you want me to do."

"There's a problem with my identification," I say, stretching the truth just a little to make her understand that my return flight is out of my hands.

I'm not ready to tell her about Evander yet because what would I say? That I picked up a stranger four days ago, and now I feel responsible for him? To make this story believable, I should add that I'm falling for this man I just met.

"You've been my assistant for five years, Jinelle. If someone knows Indie Inkpot better than I do, it's you."

"But I need you here," she says, dry-heaving on the order end.

"I wouldn't ask this of you if I wasn't certain you could handle it," I say softly. "Since I won't be able to fly home, I'll have to drive across the country," I say, pressing my lips together as I prepare myself for another round of retaliation.

Jinelle takes a deep breath and I brace myself. "That's going to take you days. Plus, it's super dangerous. A beautiful woman traveling by herself. You know how many horror movies start like that? And don't get me started on unsolved murders."

She doesn't give me another chance.

"I'm not alone," I say, a grin forming on my lips when I watch Evander walk in my direction with two paper cups.

"Carena, I don't know what's going on, but I'm coming to get you," Jinelle replies, and I can hear her keys jingle in the background. "Don't move."

"No need. I'm fine. To be honest, I've never felt better," I answer, grabbing the cup that Evander holds towards me. "And you're not alone either. You have an amazing team at your disposal. I'll be back in the office before you know it."

"You don't sound fine. You haven't taken a day off since the opening. And now, all of a sudden, you take an entire weekend off, vanish from the face of the earth for another two days, and now you add even more. Now tell me again I shouldn't worry about you."

Yeah, she has a point.

"I'll send you photos," I say, coming up with the only solution I can think of.

"And you keep your tracker on," she warns, and I hear her fingers tapping against her phone. "If I don't see you moving for longer than ten minutes, I'll call the police."

I laugh. "Got it," I reply, taking a warm sip from my latte. "You got this."

"You'll be the judge of that once you're back," Jinelle says nervously. "Remember, this was your idea. You can't fire me if I mess up."

"I promise I won't fire you," I reply before hanging up.

"Everything okay?" Evander asks, staring at the drink in his hand as if this is his very first coffee in his life and he doesn't know what to think of it.

"Jinelle is going to crush it," I smile, moving onto my tippy toes to kiss his lips.

"Since we can't fly, what do we do now?" Evander asks, biting the inside of his lip.

I grin at him. "We travel the good old way: by road."

THIRTY-FOUR

EVANDER

"Wouldn't it be easier to collect magnets like normal people do?" I ask, watching Carena survey our surroundings for any onlookers.

"Four states in, and you're getting cold feet now?"

No, this has nothing to do with cold feet. I'm rock hard for her as my eyes follow her every move while she tries to find the perfect spot.

"Let's just find a hotel and call it a night," I grunt, stumbling after her.

I forgot how exhausting it is to be human. My knees pop every time I get up, and my back hurts from all the driving.

"A deal is a deal," she replies, grinning over her shoulder at me.

I don't think she realizes how beautiful she is, and I'm not talking about her long, dark hair, her amber eyes, and her perfectly round ass. I'm talking about that light for adventure I saw in her eyes as a child, which reignited the moment we walked away from the ticket counter.

Watching Carena grow from a child into an independent powerhouse is something I'll never forget. Even though she's still unaware of her own resilience and how much she shaped the lives of the people around her, I am because I'm one of those individuals.

She gave me hope that not every human seeks power and that, despite her broken heart, she goes above and beyond for the people she loves.

I'm lucky to count myself as one of them—I might say I'm the luckiest since I'm about to make her beg for more while I thrust into her, marking another state we had sex in off our list.

"Are you already tired of me?" Carena asks, dragging her pants down to display her beautifully curved ass in its full glory.

Curling my hands into fists to restrain myself from jumping her, I look around one last time before unbuckling my pants to free my cock.

"Never, Darling," I growl as I grab her hair and press her face against a massive rock near our rental car.

"Don't hold back," she whimpers as she bucks against me, her neediness dripping down my cock as I drag the tip through her folds.

I know she likes it, rough and risky.

"I wouldn't dare," I grunt, pressing into her, and for a split second, I feel my other consciousness trying to gain control over my body. Biting my lip, I fight the feeling of my mind slipping out of my inner grasp, and with the next thrust, I regain control.

Everything I told her about my past was true—the way I was created, losing Alia, being exiled, and how I ended up in her grandma's hands.

But there's one vital part I swore would die with my djinn ability once I'm freed.

It was foolish to think that I'll ever be free again, and all I can do now is hope that *he* doesn't find me.

ARE YOU READY FOR MORE?

ABOUT THE AUTHOR

C.K. Franziska is the author of the finished A *Speck of Darkness* series, and her second series, The Crymzon Chronicles. She is the wife of a traveler, as well as the mother of two mini versions of herself and way too many pets. In her spare time, she is also a photographer, traveler, full-time entertainer, and animal lover. She does her best writing at night, at the beach listening to the waves, or while camping. C.K. loves to play make-believe, transporting readers to a place where the heroes have to step out of the seemingly endless cycle of family curses, where the magic is as beautiful and untamable as we think, and where every person deserves to be celebrated.

Made in the USA
Columbia, SC
25 September 2024

42395023R00150